Jenny was pregnant.

Mike looked down at her and the flash in her blue eyes did nothing to ease the anger bubbling and frothing inside him. It didn't help to know that even as furious as he was, he could still look at her and need her.

"No matter what you think," she said tightly, "I didn't trick you. I didn't set up a *trap* to catch the mighty and elusive Mike Ryan."

"Well, since you're so honest," he ground out, "I'll just believe you, okay?"

"You should but you won't," she told him, shaking her head, sending those curls that drove him crazy into a wild dance about her head. She underlined each of her words with a determined tap of her index finger against his chest. "Do you really think I would trap a man who doesn't want me? I've got more self-respect than that, thanks."

Jenny stood facing him, her chin lifted, eyes narrowed and hot with banked fury. She looked beautiful and strong and it took everything he had to fight down the urge to grab her and pull her in close. Jenny Marshall got to him like no one else ever had and he hated admitting that, even to himself.

* * *

A Baby for the Boss is part of the Pregnant by the Boss trilogy—Three business partners find love—and fatherhood—where they least expect it.

Dear Reader,

I love connected books. In this second book in the Pregnant by the Boss trilogy, you'll get to know Mike Ryan and Jenny Marshall.

The fun part is, you already met these two in *Having Her Boss's Baby*. For me, connecting books gives me the opportunity to delve deeper into characters that only played a small part in a previous book. Plus, I get to revisit the previous hero and heroine and keep up with what's happening in their lives!

In *A Baby for the Boss*, you'll see Mike and Jenny snarl at each other and eventually give in to the undeniable connection between them. But there's a lot in each of their pasts that they'll have to overcome if they want to reach out and grab the shiny future waiting for them.

I really hope you love this book. I had such a good time with these two! Right now, I'm at work on book three in the trilogy and I think the last Ryan brother might be the most stubborn of all.

Please visit me on Facebook and Twitter. Let me know what you think of my books—and even what you'd like to see in future stories! Until then, I wish you great friends, much love and good books!

Happy reading!

Maureen

A BABY FOR
THE BOSS

MAUREEN CHILD

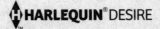

Recycling programs
for this product may
not exist in your area.

ISBN-13: 978-0-373-73434-4

A Baby for the Boss

Printed in U.S.A.

www.Harlequin.com

Maureen Child writes for the Harlequin Desire line and can't imagine a better job.

A seven-time finalist for a prestigious Romance Writers of America RITA® Award, Maureen is the author of more than one hundred romance novels. Her books regularly appear on bestseller lists and have won several awards, including a Prism Award, a National Readers' Choice Award, a Colorado Romance Writers Award of Excellence and a Golden Quill Award.

One of her books, *The Soul Collector*, was made into a CBS TV movie starring Melissa Gilbert, Bruce Greenwood and Ossie Davis. If you look closely, in the last five minutes of the movie you'll spot Maureen, who was an extra in the last scene.

Maureen believes that laughter goes hand in hand with love, so her stories are always filled with humor. The many letters she receives assure her that her readers love to laugh as much as she does. Maureen Child is a native Californian but has recently moved to the mountains of Utah.

Books by Maureen Child

Harlequin Desire

The Fiancée Caper
After Hours with Her Ex
Triple the Fun
Double the Trouble

Pregnant by the Boss trilogy

Having Her Boss's Baby
A Baby for the Boss

Visit the Author Profile page
at Harlequin.com, or
maureenchild.com, for more titles.

To Sarah and Dan—
Ten years is something to celebrate
As we celebrate the two of you every day
We love you

One

"I don't trust her." Mike Ryan drummed his fingertips on his desktop and glared at his younger brother.

"Yeah," Sean said on a laugh. "You've made that clear for months. What *isn't* clear is why. She's a terrific artist, meets her deadlines, is easy to get along with and a hell of a baker—she's always bringing goodies in for everyone. So how about you tell me what Jenny Marshall ever did that you're so against her."

Scowling, Mike gritted his teeth and shifted his gaze to the view out his office window. Even in Southern California, January gardens looked a little grim. The backyard of the Victorian mansion that served as Celtic Knot Gaming's office boasted dry, brown grass, leafless trees and empty flower beds. The sky was studded with gray clouds and a cold wind swept in off the ocean to rattle those bare tree limbs.

Still, looking at that dismal view was better than drawing up a mental image of Jenny Marshall. As unwilling as he was, though, that picture of her flashed across his brain. She was a damn munchkin, only standing about five foot two, but that tiny body was really packed well. She had curves that made Mike's mouth water every time he saw her—especially since he already knew just what those curves looked like *naked*. One more reason he tried to avoid running into her.

Her short blond hair was a mass of curls that ended at her jawline, stirring up a grown man's idle daydreams into fantasies of hot, sweaty nights. Instantly, he forced his mind away from the images of naked Jenny and instead thought of her eyes. As blue as the sky, bright with lies—and once, glazed with passion—for him.

Okay, that's enough of that, he told himself firmly.

"I've got my reasons," he muttered, not bothering to look at his brother again.

Sean had no clue that Mike and Jenny had met long before she was hired at Celtic Knot and there was no reason for that to change.

"Fine." Sean blew out a breath. "Always were a hardhead. Anyway, doesn't matter what the reasons are. You, me and Brady already decided this."

"Brady's in Ireland."

"Yep," Sean said, then added, "ain't technology great? You do remember the meeting we had over webcam? The one where we *all* decided who would do which hotel?"

"I remember."

"Good. Because Jenny's in her office right now, working on the designs for the River Haunt hotel." Sean met his brother's gaze. "She's already coming up with some great stuff. If we switch designers at this stage, it's going to slow down everything. Besides, Jenny's good. She *earned* this."

Mike scowled and bit back any further argument because it just wouldn't do any good. Sean was right: the plans had been made. He couldn't change them now. All of the artists for the company had already been assigned their work schedules. Most of them were finishing up the graphics for the next game to be released in the coming summer. So Jenny was the only logical choice.

Didn't mean he had to like it.

But there were deadlines to meet and no one knew that better than Mike. He, his brother and their friend Brady Finn had begun this gaming company when they were still in college. Their first game had been short on art and long on mystery and action. It had taken off faster than any of them had hoped and by the time they graduated from college, they were all millionaires.

They'd plowed their money back into the company they called Celtic Knot and within six months had released a bigger, more sophisticated game. They built a reputation for action games based on ancient Irish legends and superstitions, and their fan base swelled.

They'd bought this old Victorian in Long Beach, California, as their home base and hired the very best computer programmers, and digital and graphic artists.

They'd won awards and had legions of fans waiting for the release of their next game. And now, they were growing in another direction.

They were buying three hotels and revamping them into perfect role-playing venues for guests. Each hotel would be modeled after one of their top-selling games. The first, Fate Castle, was in Ireland. The modifications had just recently been completed and the hotel would be open and welcoming guests in March. The second, River Haunt, was in Nevada on the Colorado River and was just waiting for Mike to step up and get the renovations moving forward.

But how the hell could he do that while working one-on-one with Jenny Marshall? Answer: he couldn't. But he wasn't prepared to go into all of the reasons why with Sean. Instead, he'd simply go to Jenny. Convince her to back off this project. She was probably in no more hurry to work with him than he was with her. If she went to Sean herself and asked to be replaced, there wouldn't be a problem. Mike would offer her a raise. Or a bonus. A woman like her would jump at a chance for that—and he'd be able to get on with the hotel transformation.

"Meantime," Sean said, loudly enough to snap Mike's attention back to the moment, "I'm still talking to the toy company about the line of collectibles they're proposing based on our gaming characters."

"What do the lawyers say?" Mike asked.

"Plenty," Sean admitted. "And most of it I can't understand. I swear they teach these people to speak in tongues when they're in law school."

"Agreed. How much did you get out of it?"

Sean crossed his legs, ankle on knee. "Enough to know that if they up their offer on the licensing fee, this could be a really good thing for us."

"I don't know… Toys?"

"Not toys. Collectibles," Sean corrected. "I called Brady this morning and he's on board. So think about this, Mike. At the next gaming convention we not only have the games to push, but the collectibles. We can spin that off to board games even, for people not interested in video games."

Mike laughed shortly and leaned back in his chair. "There aren't many people uninterested in games."

"Okay, true. But we're pushing into the hotel industry, giving people a chance to live their favorite games. We could take that another step," Sean said, slapping one hand down on Mike's desk. "We can sponsor our own conventions."

"What?" Surprised, Mike just stared at him.

Sean grinned. "Think about it. Hell, Comic-Con started out small and look at them now. We could hold Celtic Knot Con—an entire convention centered around our games and products. We can host tournaments, offer prizes. Costume contests. Hell, we could run a contest offering a contract to whoever comes up with the best new beast to use in one of our games."

"Did you go surfing this morning?"

Sean stopped. "What's that got to do with anything?"

"That water's cold, probably froze a few brain cells."

"Funny."

"Don't you think we've got enough going on right now? The latest game came out in December, and the sequel to 'Fate Castle' hits this summer, not to mention the hotel business."

"Okay, we're busy," Sean allowed. "We want to *stay* busy, we have to keep thinking, expanding. Our business is based on the fans. On the way they feel connected to the scenarios we create. If we give them more, offer them other ways to connect, to feel a part of the world they love, that can only benefit us."

Mike thought about it for a minute. He could see the enthusiasm on his brother's face and knew that Sean was at least partly right. Continuing to build their brand would only solidify their position in the marketplace.

The castle hotel in Ireland already had a waiting list six months long and they hadn't even opened yet. That told Mike there was a huge market for just what Sean was describing. And little brother was right about something else, too.

"We'll talk to Brady about your convention idea—that may be a good way to go."

"Whoa." Sean grinned. "This is a moment. Maybe I should hunt up a photographer."

Mike laughed. "Okay, fine. I think you're onto something. On the collectibles, I'm on board. Tell the lawyers to work up the company's licensing offer and then we'll sign."

"Already did," Sean said.

"Sure of yourself, weren't you?"

"Damn right."

Amused, Mike said, "Okay, well, you're right about the other stuff, too. The role-playing, the contests. Ireland's too hard for a lot of people to get to. The grounds on the hotel in Nevada aren't big enough for us to hold tournaments on any kind of real scale. So the hotel in Wyoming will have to be the base for that kind of growth."

"Just what I was thinking," Sean said. "It's on a hundred and fifty acres, with lakes and forests. It's perfect for the kind of thing I'm talking about."

"Then it's handy you're in charge of that one, isn't it?"

"Also what I was thinking," Sean said with a quick, smug smile.

It was the smug part that had Mike suggesting, "You should go to Wyoming. Check it out in person."

Sean snorted. "Sure. That'll happen. It's *January*, Mike. It's snowing there. Like crazy cold snowing." He shivered. "No, thank you. Look, we bought the property in Ireland by checking it out online and that worked great."

"Yeah, but—"

"I've talked to the Realtor, had her make videos of everything. The inn itself needs a lot of work, but the property is perfect and that's more important, right?"

"Yeah, but—"

"You take care of yours and I'll take care of mine. No worries, I'll go look around in a few months, *before* we start the design stage." Sean stood up and looked down at Mike. "Right now, though, I'm dealing with the big Game Con in Chicago next month. And I've got the art on 'Banshee Screams' to oversee. I'll get to Wyoming," he said. "But it can wait until summer…" Shaking his head, he laughed and headed for the door. "A surfer. In the snow. Yeah. That'll work."

Mike frowned after him. Brady was happy as hell, working and living in Ireland with his wife and new baby son. Sean was busy making plans to be a happy, surfing megalomaniac. So, it was only Mike staring at nothing but trouble. It would take at least six months to refit the Nevada hotel. And since he couldn't find a way to get her off the project, that meant a hell of a lot of time spent with Jenny Marshall.

A woman who had already lied to him once.

Yeah. This was gonna be great.

Jenny Marshall poured herself a glass of white wine and sat down in an overstuffed chair, ordering herself to relax. But she didn't take orders well, not even from herself. Curling her feet up under her, Jenny looked out the window at the neighbor kids playing basketball in the driveway across the street.

The duplex she rented was old and small. Built in the 1940s, it sat on a narrow street a few blocks from the beach. The rent was too high, but the place itself was cozy, close to work and less generic than some cramped apartment. Here, she could garden and go to block parties and buy Girl Scout cookies and football pizzas from the kids who lived on the street. Here, Jenny felt that she was…connected. A part of things. And for a woman alone, that feeling was priceless.

She took a sip of her wine and shifted her gaze to the front yard, where bare trees clattered in the wind. Twilight fell over the neighborhood in a soft lavender glow and lamplight began blooming in her neighbors' windows. Relaxation still eluded her, but with everything she had on her mind that really wasn't a surprise.

Between her work on the upcoming game from Celtic Knot and the designs she was working on for the River Haunt hotel, there was plenty to think about. She did love her job and was grateful for it. Especially since one of her bosses would like nothing better than to fire her—or to see her drop into a black hole and simply disappear.

She frowned into her glass and tried to ignore the pain of regret that clutched at her heart. It hadn't been easy, working with Mike Ryan for the past several months. Every time they were in the same room together, she felt hostility coming off him in waves so thick it nearly choked her. The man was hard-hearted, stubborn, unreasonable and…still the one man who made her insides quiver.

She lifted her glass of wine in a toast to her own stupidity.

Seriously, hadn't she learned her lesson more than a year ago? When they met that night in Phoenix, it had been magic, pure and simple. And, like any good fairy tale, the magic had lasted exactly one night. Then Prince Charming had turned into an ogre and Jenny's proverbial glass slippers were flip-flops again.

It had all started out so well, too. The night before a big gaming convention in Phoenix, Jenny had met a tall, gorgeous man with a wicked smile and eyes as blue as a summer sky. They had a drink together in the bar, then had dinner, then took a walk and finally had ended up in her room at the convention hotel. She'd never done that before—gone to bed with a man she barely knew. But that night, everything had been…different. From the moment she met Mike, she'd felt as if she had somehow only been *waiting* for him to walk into her life. Which, she could admit now, was absolutely ridiculous. But that night… Jenny had allowed her heart to rule her head. She'd given in to the rush of attraction, that *zing* of something special that she'd only ever felt for him. And by morning, Jenny knew she'd made a huge mistake.

Sighing, she laid her head against the back of the chair, closed her eyes and drifted back to the moment when the floor had opened up beneath her feet. The morning *after* the best night of her life.

Mike pulled her close and Jenny laid her head on his chest, listening to the steady beat of his heart. Her body was loose and languid from a long night of loving. Dawn streaked the morning sky with pale rose and gold and she was nowhere near wanting to get out of bed.

This was so unlike her, she thought, smiling to herself. She didn't do one-night stands and never with a veritable stranger. But she couldn't regret any of it. From the moment she'd met Mike, she'd felt as if she'd known him forever. She didn't even know his last name, yet she felt closer to him at that moment than she had to anyone else.

"Really hate to move from this spot," Mike said, "but I've got to get down to the convention floor early."

"I know. Me, too." Jenny cuddled in closer. "My uncle needs me to set up his booth. He can't get here until to-morrow, so..."

Mike ran one hand up and down her back and his fingertips felt like tiny sparks of heat against her skin.

"Yeah?" Mike asked, his voice low and slow and lazy. "Who's your uncle?"

"Hmm?" She was nearly hypnotized by the slide of his fingers and the deep rumble of his voice. "Oh. Hank Snyder," she whispered. "He owns Snyder Arts."

Mike suddenly went still. His hand dropped from her back and she felt a hard shift in the lovely little glow they'd been sharing. Then there was a physical shift as Mike pushed to a sitting position and rolled Jenny right off his chest.

She plopped onto the bed and stared up at him. "What?"

"Hank Snyder?" Mike jumped out of bed and stood staring down at her with a wild, dark gleam in his eyes, sharp as a knife blade. With the morning light stream-ing in through the window behind him, he looked like a naked avenging angel.

The haze in her mind was clearing and a cold, sinking sensation opened in the pit of her stomach. Slowly, she sat up and tugged the blankets over her breasts. Pushing one hand through her hair, she shoved blond curls out of her eyes and met his hard gaze with a look of confusion. "What's wrong?" she asked. "Do you know my uncle?"

He snorted. "Wow. That's really good. The little hint of innocence in your voice? Nice touch."

Completely confused now, she shook her head. People should not be expected to be coherent in the morning before several cups of coffee. "Innocence? What?"

"Oh, drop it," Mike snapped and stalked across the room to snatch up his clothes. He dragged them on as he talked, flicking her quick, icy glances. "Gotta say, you were good."

"What are you talking about?" The sheet where he'd been lying only a moment ago was rapidly cooling and she shivered in response. "Good at what? You're not making sense."

"Sure. You're confused." Mike nodded. "You know, I bought the whole act last night, but trying to keep it up now, when I know who you are, is only pissing me off."

She didn't have the first clue what he was so angry about, but her own temper was beginning to boil in self-defense. How could they have gone from lovemaking, to snuggling, to spitting ice at each other all in the blink of an eye?

"Will you just tell me what's going on?"

"What I don't get is how you knew I'd be in the bar last night." He pulled his long-sleeved white shirt on and buttoned it with an almost eerie calm that belied the fury in his voice and eyes.

"I didn't know—heck, I didn't even know I was going to be in the bar last night until just before I went in."

"Sure. Your uncle," Mike said, nodding. "He had to have planned all this for you anyway."

"What does Uncle Hank have to do with us?"

He laughed but there was no charm or humor in it. "Everything, sweetheart, and we both know it. Snyder

Arts has been trying to get us to incorporate their programs into our games for the past year and a half." His
gaze dropped to her chest, then lifted to her eyes again.
"Looks like Ol' Hank finally decided to pull out the big
guns."

Every word Mike said echoed weirdly in her mind
until at last, Jenny understood what he meant. What he
was accusing her of. Anger leaped into a full boil in the
pit of her stomach. Her heart pounded crazily and she
felt as if she couldn't catch her breath. Her mind racing,
Jenny practically leaped out of bed, preferring to meet
her accuser on her feet. She held the blanket up in front
of her like a shield that could somehow protect her from
the ice in his eyes.

"You think my uncle sent me here to have sex with
you?" God, she could barely force the words past her
tight throat. "So I could convince you to use his arts
program?"

"That about sums it up," Mike said flatly.

Jenny's brain burned. She was torn between insult,
fury and complete humiliation. Instantly, images of the
night before streamed through her mind like a movie on
fast-forward. She saw him, over her, staring into her eyes
as his body claimed hers. She saw herself, straddling
him, taking him deep inside her. And she felt in that flash
of heat the pleasure, the sense of completion his every
touch caused. Then the mind movie ended abruptly, and
she was here, in this sunlit room, staring at a stranger
who now knew her body intimately, but her heart and
soul not at all.

"Who the hell do you think you are?" she asked, voice
trembling.

"Mike Ryan."

She staggered at the name. Mike Ryan. One of the owners of Celtic Knot. Jenny knew their work, knew the art and graphic design that went into every one of their games. She'd admired them for years, had hoped to one day work for them—which wouldn't happen now. Not only did he clearly think she was a spy—and oh yes, a whore—but she couldn't imagine herself working for a man who made snap decisions with zero thought behind them.

"Uh-huh," he said, nodding as if he'd just had every one of his suspicions verified. "So you do know me."

"Now," she said. "I didn't last night. Not when I met you. Not when we..." She pushed one hand through her hair and kept clutching the blanket with the other. Best not to think about everything they'd done because she'd do something completely stupid like blush, for heaven's sake. With her fair skin, the moment she was embarrassed, her cheeks lit up like a red light at an intersection.

"And I'm supposed to take your word for that," he said.

Her gaze sharpened and narrowed on him. "It seems you don't need anything but your own suspicions to make up your mind. You've already decided who and what I am, why should I argue with you over it?"

"You know, playing the outraged innocent isn't nearly as convincing as the seductress I met last night."

She sucked in a gulp of air and fed the flames burning in her belly. "You arrogant, conceited, smug bastard."

One dark eyebrow winged up and a look of pure male amusement tugged at the corners of his mouth. "Doing better now. The outrage almost looks real."

Her heart pounded so hard in her chest it was a won-

der he couldn't hear it. She half expected her heart to crash right through her rib cage. "This isn't an act, you jackass. Think about it. I didn't seduce you. You approached me in the bar. And nobody forced you into my bed. As I remember it you came willingly enough."

"Several times," he said, playing on her words just to irritate her further.

It worked.

"That's it. I don't have to listen to any more of your paranoid ramblings. Get out of my room." She swung one hand toward the door and stabbed the air with her index finger.

He grabbed his black jacket off a nearby chair and shrugged it on. "Oh, I'm going. No worries there. I wouldn't stay if you begged me to."

"That's not gonna happen."

He snorted again, a particularly annoying, insulting sound. Striding across the room to the door, he stopped before he opened it and looked back over his shoulder at her. "Tell your uncle I said nice try, but no cigar. Celtic Knot won't be doing a deal with him no matter how many attractive nieces he tosses into my bed."

Jenny picked up a wineglass from the room service tray they'd shared the night before and hurled it at him. He was through the door and out before the glass shattered against the wood to lie in splinters on the floor.

Jenny sighed and took another sip of her wine. She hadn't thought to even see Mike Ryan again, but then six months later, his brother, Sean, had offered her a job that was simply too good to pass up. The chance to work on the kind of art she loved was worth the risk of being around Mike every day. And frankly, by being on-site every day, she was silently telling Mike Ryan that what he'd done hadn't hurt her. Hadn't crushed her. Of course that was a big, fat lie, but he didn't have to know that. Working at Celtic Knot was a dream that only occasionally became a nightmare when she was forced to deal with Mike.

Of course now, the nightmare would be a 24/7 thing for the next few months. Yes, she was excited about being the artist to design the murals for the River Haunt hotel. But having to work one-on-one with Mike was going to make it all so much more grueling than it should have been. Still, she wouldn't back off. Oh, Jenny knew that Mike wanted her off the project, but this was too big an opportunity for her to turn tail and run. Especially, she reminded herself, since she'd done nothing wrong.

He was the one who had plenty to apologize for. He was the one who'd insulted her, humiliated her and then stomped off without so much as listening to her side of the story.

So why should *she* be the one to pay a price?

The knock on her door interrupted her thoughts and she told herself, if it was a salesman, she'd buy whatever he was selling out of simple gratitude.

She opened the door and stared up into Mike Ryan's blazing blue eyes. Without waiting to be invited in, he pushed his way past her and marched into her apartment with all the determination of Grant taking Richmond.

With little else to do but accept the inevitable, Jenny closed the door. "Well, do come in," she said, every word dripping with sarcasm. "Make yourself at home."

Features grim, eyes the color of a lake frozen over, he said, "We need to talk."

Two

Mike stopped in the middle of the room, turned and just looked at her. She wore a pale green T-shirt and faded, curve-hugging jeans with a hole at the knee. Her small, narrow feet were bare but for the pale pink nail polish. Her hair was a rumpled mass of tumbling blond curls and her wide blue eyes were fixed on him warily. She looked good. Too damned good, and that was part of the problem.

Stuffing both hands into his pockets, just to keep from reaching for her, Mike deliberately looked away from Jenny and glanced around the small living room. His gaze picked out the details even as his brain reminded him not to let her distract him. Great body, beautiful eyes and kissable lips notwithstanding, he had come here for a reason and he had to keep his focus.

The duplex was old, probably one of the original beach

cottages built in the late 1930s. Jenny's home was well kept, casual and welcoming. There were overstuffed chairs covered in a flowery fabric and a love seat boasting yellow and blue stripes. Several small tables and standing brass lamps were scattered about the room, shining puddles of golden light onto the scarred but polished wood floors and the few rugs that broke up the space. The walls were painted a soft green that reminded him of spring. There were framed paintings and photographs clustered together in no discernible pattern and on one wall, there was a mural.

His gaze caught it and held. Obviously, Jenny had painted it herself and Mike had to admit that whatever else she was, the woman was also immensely talented. The mural was a scene straight out of a fairy tale—or an Irish legend. A forest, just waking up to daylight. Fog drifted across the landscape in thin gray wisps, sunlight speared through the trees to lie in a dappled pattern on the leaf-strewn ground. There was a hint of a flower-laden meadow in the distance and in the towering trees were fairies, delicate wings looking as if they would flutter any minute.

Damn it. He hated that she was this good.

"Why are you here, Mike?" Her voice was soft, but the glint in her eye was anything but.

Good question. Mike knew he probably shouldn't have come here—they hadn't been alone together since that night in Phoenix—but he had run out of options. He couldn't tell Sean why working with Jenny was a mistake—because damned if he'd let his little brother know that he'd once been taken for a ride. In more ways than one.

But Jenny knew why this wouldn't work. All he had

to do was get her to tell Sean she didn't want the job of
designing the art for the new hotel. And if Jenny herself requested that she be let out of the project, Sean
wouldn't object.

Time to get to the point so Mike could get the hell out
of this too-small house where her scent seemed to hover
in the air for the express purpose of tormenting him. "I
want you to back out of the hotel job."

She didn't even blink. "Interesting. Well, I want to be
three inches taller and have smaller boobs. Looks like
we're both doomed to disappointment."

Why the hell she would want smaller breasts was beyond him, but not the point. "We both know that working together for months is a bad idea."

"Agreed." She crossed her arms over her chest, pushing her breasts higher. "Maybe you're the one who should
quit. Switch hotels with Sean. I *like* Sean."

"Leave Sean alone," Mike ground out.

Her oh-so-casual pose evaporated and she threw her
hands high in frustration. "Please. Now you're afraid I'm
going to be paid to seduce Sean?"

"I didn't say that." Thought it, maybe. Said it, no.
All right, he admitted silently, he hadn't even thought
it. Not really.

"What exactly *are* you saying, Mike?" She plopped
both hands on her hips and the movement tightened the
fabric of her shirt against the aforementioned breasts.
Distractions, Mike told himself. *Pay no attention.*

"I'm saying leave Sean out of this," he said. "It's between you and me."

"Fine. Then *you* tell Sean he should take over the
River Haunt and you do the Wyoming place."

"No." He wasn't ready to admit defeat yet. He could

still find a way to convince Jenny that this was an impossible situation and that it was up to *her* to back off.

She shrugged again, and walked past him slowly enough that the scent of her vanilla perfume flavored the breath he took and held as she made for the chair by the wide window.

"So, since neither one of us is willing to drop out of this project, I guess we're done here," she said, plopping into the chair and lifting her wineglass for a sip.

"We are far from done." Through the window behind her, he saw the street was dark, with the dim glow of lamplight shining through a neighbor's drapes.

January nights at the beach could be cold, but here in this tiny duplex, Mike felt only the heat of being near her again. Her hair shone, her eyes glittered and her mouth curved up at one corner when she spoke. She was enjoying this, he thought, and a part of him liked that about her.

Jenny Marshall didn't back down for anyone. He'd seen her go head-to-head with older, more experienced artists, defending her designs and techniques. She held her own in meetings and wasn't afraid to fight for her vision of things. But as much as he admired those traits, he wished she wasn't currently turning her admirable qualities on *him*.

"Mike, you don't want to work with me and I don't want to work with you. But we're stuck with each other." She lifted one shoulder in a half shrug. "We'll have to make the best of it."

"Unacceptable." Shaking his head, he looked away from her because the damn lamplight made her hair shine like burnished gold. He never should have come here. It had been a bad idea and if he were smart, he'd leave right now since their argument was getting them exactly nowhere.

As he sifted through dozens of pretty much useless thoughts, his gaze fixed on the magical forest mural. It was dark, mysterious, but with the fairies in the limbs of the trees, there was a sense of playfulness amid the darkness and the longer he looked at it, the more fairies he spotted. Hiding behind leaves, beside rocks, in the water of a fast-moving stream. It was hypnotic, mystical.

He shifted to look at her. "Damn good work," he blurted, before he could stop himself.

"Thanks." Surprise flitted across her face, then vanished. "But if you're wondering, I didn't *steal* that scene from any of Celtic Knot's games."

He fired a look at her that had been known to make stone-hearted business rivals quake. Jenny wasn't fazed. "I didn't say you stole it."

"Not yet," she told him, pausing for another sip of wine. "I'm sure you'll get to it. I know very well what you think of me."

"Do you blame me?" he countered. Mike pushed one hand through his hair, then scrubbed that hand across the back of his neck. Ever since he met her, this woman had had the ability to tangle him up into knots. Even knowing she was a damn liar hadn't taken away the rush he'd felt every time he thought of her.

At work, he kept his distance, knowing it was best for everyone. Coming here, into her place, being alone with her in the lamp-lit dark was dangerous. He knew it, and still he didn't leave. Instead, he took a single step toward her and stopped because her scent clouded his mind and he couldn't afford to addle his brain any more than it already was.

"That's not a fair question," she answered. "You made up your mind about me in an instant and never once listened to any side but your own."

"What other side *was* there?" he countered. "Hell, your uncle is still running Snyder Arts."

"Oh, for God's sake," she snapped, setting her wine-glass onto the table with a harsh click.

"Tell me I'm wrong."

"How can I? He does own Snyder Arts. He doesn't own me."

"He's family." Mike shrugged.

"Yeah, and he thinks enough of me that he's never asked me to do what you continue to imply I've already done." She sucked in air, then blew it out. "Sean's never questioned my integrity."

"Sean's more trusting than I am."

"News flash," she muttered, then asked, "Would you lie and cheat for your family?"

"No, I wouldn't." Mike had grown up knowing exactly what kind of damage lies could do. As a kid, he'd promised himself he'd avoid lies and the people who told them. That's why he couldn't trust Jenny. First time he met her, she'd lied. No going back from that.

Her eyes flashed. "But you assume I would."

"Don't have to assume a damn thing," he reminded her.

"My God, you have a thick head." She huffed out a breath. "At least come up with a *new* crime to accuse me of. I didn't use you then. I'm not using you now."

"I'm pretty sure every thief claims innocence."

She pushed out of her chair, stalked toward him and was forced to tip her head back to meet his eyes. "Name me *one* thing I've stolen. Give me *one* reason you have the right to call me a thief."

"Fine," he said, staring into her eyes until he could actually see her anger churning and burning. "You haven't stolen anything that I know of. Yet. You're a prethief."

"Then why haven't you fired me or told Sean to?"

"I do my own firing," he said. "And if I ever have proof that you've betrayed us, then I will fire you so fast your head will spin. Suspicion isn't proof."

She laughed shortly and shook her head. Then she took a long step back, and folded her arms beneath those magnificent breasts. "Boy, you're really reaching. Being a prethief is like being prepregnant. Or prepublished. All that means is you're *not* something. Like I'm *not* a thief, so I'd appreciate it if you'd quit throwing accusations around that you can't back up."

Damn, the angrier she was, the hotter she got. Bright spots of color dotted her cheeks and her blue eyes were flashing dangerously. What did it say about him that her temper only fueled the need inside him?

Most of the women in his life agreed with him, smiled coyly, flirted outrageously and in general made sure they were pleasant company. Jenny didn't give a damn about any of that. She had an opinion and wasn't afraid to share it and that was just as sexy as the way her eyes glittered.

And sexy wasn't the point.

"We both know what's going on here, Jenny," he argued. "You might not want to admit it—and who could blame you—but the fact is, your uncle owns a company that would like nothing better than to have a contract with Celtic Knot. You meet me 'accidentally,' go to bed with me and try to convince me you're not colluding with your uncle?" She opened her mouth to argue, but he rushed on before she could. "Then months later, you come to work for us, grab a job as head designer."

"I didn't 'grab' anything," she snapped. "Sean came to me and offered me the job."

He'd never told Sean about his time with Jenny. Maybe if he had, his younger brother wouldn't have hired her in the first place. Which, Mike was forced to admit, would have been a damn shame. As much as she managed to irritate him, she was a hell of an artist.

"Sean asked, but you took it." He tipped his head to one side and studied her. "So the question is, why? You miss me? Or are you some kind of corporate spy now?"

"Now I'm a spy? Wow," she said, slowly shaking her head. "Paranoia reaches new heights."

He snorted. "I'm not paranoid if you really are a spy."

"You're amazing."

"So it's been said."

She threw her hands up. "There's no talking to you. So think whatever you want," she told him, voice as icy as her eyes were hot. "You have from the beginning."

"Right. When we met at the gaming con in Phoenix. Another coincidence?" His eyebrow lifted. "You just happened to be at my hotel?"

"Or," she countered, "you arrogant jackass, *you* happened to be at *my* hotel."

Surprise almost had him laughing. Almost. But she was too furious and he was too sure he was right. There was nothing funny about being cheated. Lied to. Old memories of his mother crying, his father shamefaced, rose up in his mind, and Mike deliberately quashed them. Not the time or the place for memories, other than the ones he and Jenny had created the first time she'd lied to him.

"Right. I went looking for you that night."

"You're the one who approached me in the bar," she reminded him. "Not the other way around."

"You were beautiful. And alone." And somehow she had looked insulated, cut off, as if she'd been alone so long that she hadn't expected anything else from her life. Intrigued, Mike had watched her sip a single glass of wine for nearly an hour, as bar patrons came and went. As the bartender flirted with her and she ignored him, apparently oblivious to her own allure.

Mike wasn't unaware, though. She was tiny, making a man want to step up and be her protector. She was beautiful, making a man want to see her smile to know what that smile would do to her eyes. And she had so many curves in all the right places, *any* man would have wanted to get her out of the short red dress and high, needle-thin heels she had worn.

How the hell could he have resisted her?

She flushed at the unexpected compliment and he watched, fascinated, as a stain of deep rose filled her cheeks. She looked away from him then as if hoping to regain her sense of balance. He knew how that felt because damned if he didn't feel off his game every time he was around her.

"Look," she said, her voice cool and even, "the past is done. All we have now is the present and the future." Lifting her gaze to his, she said, "I'm not walking away from the hotel project. Not only is it my *job*, but it's going to be fun."

"Not how it looks from where I'm standing," he muttered.

"Well that's how I'm looking at it. So you can either deal or switch hotels with Sean."

"You don't make the calls in *my* business," he pointed out, irritated that she could try and order him off his own damn project.

"Sean put me in charge of the art design," she argued. "Not you. If you have a problem with that, talk to him."

"I did." He pushed one hand through his hair and started pacing, more to get away from the scent of her than because he needed to move. "But he doesn't know what happened in Phoenix so he doesn't get it."

"So tell him," she shot back. "If you're so sure I'm a thief and untrustworthy, tell him and let him fire me."

"I'm not telling him that I let myself get used by a woman who looks more like one of the fairies she paints than she does a damn spy."

"Wow. Thief and spy," she mused. "I'm really notorious, aren't I?"

"Why the hell else would you come and work for my company if it wasn't to be a spy for your uncle? You had to know that we'd be thrown together and clearly that thought didn't bother you. The only answer I can come up with is you're still trying to use me—now *us*, for your uncle's sake." That one question had been simmering inside his brain for months. Ever since the day he'd walked into the graphic design room and seen the woman he hadn't been able to stop thinking about sitting at one of the computers.

Damn it, he *wanted* her to convince him he was wrong, that his thoughts were baseless. He wanted to know that she really was the woman she'd seemed to be when he first met her.

"Listen up, you unbelievably suspicious...*man*. I took that job in spite of you, not *because* of you. Sean offered me a great position doing something I'm damn good at and I should have turned it down because I might see *you*?"

"I don't buy it. I think I'm the reason you took the job," Mike said, his gaze spearing into hers from across the narrow room. "You were hoping to get me into bed again."

Her head jerked back as if she'd been slapped. Gulping a deep breath, she muttered, "You pompous, arrogant... You know, sex with you wasn't *that* good."

He laughed shortly. "Now I know you're lying. It's amazing what a talent you have for it."

"Get out," she said flatly, holding up both hands toward him as if warding him off. "Just get out of my house and go away. Far, far away."

Mike shook his head.

"That night we had was incredible," he said. "And I know you felt the same way."

"Please."

His body churning, his brain racing, Mike stalked back to her, grabbed her and pulled her in close. "Since you asked so nicely..."

He kissed her, drowning in the taste and scent and feel of her. Not since that hot, amazing night in Phoenix had Mike felt so completely *right* about anything. She squirmed halfheartedly against him for a second or two, as if she might actually try to deny what was happening between them as thoroughly as she'd lied about their past.

But then the moment was gone, hesitation evaporated and she wrapped herself around him, arms locked about his neck, her short, shapely legs hooked around his waist. His hands dropped to the curve of her behind and held her there, tight against the erection straining and pulsing with the need to be buried inside her.

Had he known what would happen when he'd decided to come here tonight? Had he guessed that he wouldn't be able to deny himself—as he had for months—the sheer glory of her body? Didn't matter, he told himself as his tongue swept into the heat of her mouth. Nothing mattered but the now. The feel of her surrounding him, pulling him deeper.

No other woman had ever affected him like this. It was as if his brain and his body weren't even linked. He knew this was a bad idea, but his body just didn't give a damn. All it wanted…needed was her. One more night of being in her, on her, under her.

He tore his mouth free of hers, then shifted to taste her at the pulse beat in her throat. Her heart hammered in time with his own.

"Mike…" She sucked in a gulp of air and shivered in his arms when he nibbled at her skin. "We really shouldn't do this—"

"Yeah, I know," he whispered against her neck. "Do you care?"

"No."

"Good." His grip on her tightened and she ground her hips against him, her heels digging into the small of his back. He groaned and hissed in a breath. "You're killin' me here."

She lifted her gaze to his and a slow, sensual smile curved her mouth. "Killing you, not really the plan."

"There's a plan?"

That smile widened as she leaned in and kissed him. "Oh, yeah."

He shook his head. "I don't know why…"

"Why what?" she murmured, then gasped as his hands kneaded her behind.

"Why it's *you* who does this to me," he said on another groan as his mind shut down and his body simply
took the lead.

"Ditto," she whispered, then kissed the side of his
neck, trailing her lips and the edges of her teeth along
his skin.

"Oh, yeah." He held her tighter to his groin. "Bedroom. Where?"

"Down the hall," she whispered, her breath blowing
hot against the dampness of his skin. "Hurry."

"On that." Thankfully, her place was so small, it didn't
take him long to carry her into the bedroom. Like the
rest of the apartment, the room was tiny. A double bed,
covered by a brightly colored quilt, stood against one
wall. Pale yellow curtains were parted over a window
that opened onto the backyard where a soft, violet glow
heralded twilight.

A narrow cushioned chair sat alongside the bed, and
the dresser on the opposite wall boasted a wide mirror
that reflected the two of them as Mike dropped her onto
the mattress.

He stretched out over her, braced himself on his hands
at either side of her head and bent to kiss her. Jenny's
hands scraped up and down his arms as her mouth fused
to his. God, she tasted good. Almost as good as she felt.

Quickly, he pulled her shirt up and off, then sent it
sailing to a corner of the room. With just her lacy white
bra standing between him and what he most wanted,
Mike couldn't wait. He flicked the clasp open, then slid
the straps down her arms. His gaze locked on the feast
that was Jenny Marshall. He groaned and bent his head
to take first one hardened nipple and then the other into
his mouth.

Her hands fisted in his hair, holding him to her as his teeth and tongue lavished attention on those full, beautiful breasts. She came up off the bed when he suckled her and the groan that shot from her throat seemed to roll around them, echoing off the walls and ceiling.

Not enough, his brain screamed at him. *More. Take more.*

He dropped his hands to the snap and zipper of her jeans and undid them quickly. With her help as she wriggled eagerly beneath him, he scraped the worn denim down her legs, taking the flimsy scrap of lace panties with them. Then she was there before him, naked, willing, as desperately hungry for this as he was, and Mike couldn't wait another second to claim her.

"Too many clothes," she muttered as she ran her hands over his chest in frantic strokes, unbuttoning his shirt as she went, tearing at the tiny white buttons, muttering, "I hate buttons, why are there so many buttons?"

"No more buttons," he said tightly as he shrugged out of his shirt and tossed it over his shoulder. "I'll make a note."

"Good, good." Her fingers stroked his skin then and each tiny stroke of her nails felt like fire dragged over flesh, burning, branding.

He took a breath and held it, calling on every ounce of control he'd ever possessed, knowing it wouldn't be enough. If he didn't have her soon, the top of his head would explode. But Mike dragged it out. It had been too long since he'd had his hands on her and he wanted to savor the moment.

He ran his hands down her body, breast to the heat of her and back up to her breast again. He explored every curve, every line, and with each caress he gave her, she reached for him, fingers grabbing at his shoulders, trying to pull him in closer, tighter. Her hips arched and rocked when he dipped one hand to the heart of her and cupped her heat.

"Mike!" Her head dug back into the mattress as she lifted her hips into his touch. "If you don't get out of those slacks and come to me soon, I—" She broke off, dragged in air and whimpered when he drove first one finger and then two into her damp heat. "Mike, please!"

He worked her, driving himself and her to the edge of control and beyond. It took everything he had to keep from giving her just what she wanted. Just what he wanted. But first, he would torment them both. It had been a long year and a half.

His thumb brushed over that one tiny bud of sensation and the deliberate caress had her shout his name. Again and again, he touched her, deeply, outside, inside, across that sensitive piece of flesh until she groaned and whispered broken pleas for a release that he kept just out of reach. Her eyes glazed over, her body continued to twist and writhe, chasing a climax he refused to give her too early.

Then he couldn't bear it anymore. Pulling away from her, he stood, stripped out of the rest of his clothes and kept his gaze locked with hers as he did. She licked her lips, rocked her hips again in silent invitation and held up her arms to welcome him.

"Almost," he murmured and she groaned again, frustrated. Until he knelt on the floor and dragged her body toward him. When she was close enough, he covered her heat with his mouth and felt the crash of the climax that slammed into her. She reached down, held him to her as her body convulsed. His tongue flicked over her, into her and he tasted her as she exploded, crying out his name over and over like a mantra designed to prolong the pleasure rocking her.

When she was limp and her gasping breaths were shuddering in and out of her lungs, he joined her on the bed and she rolled into his arms. One leg tossed across his hip, she brushed the tip of him against her heat and Mike almost lost it. Then she slid her hand down and her fingers wrapped around his hard length, working his flesh as expertly as he had hers.

He hissed in a breath, squeezed his eyes shut for a moment and then opened them again to look down into hers. "Tell me you've got condoms."

"Yeah, oh, yeah. Bedside drawer." She wiggled her hips, grinding her body against his. "Hurry."

"Right." Mike didn't think about why she had condoms. About the other men she must have invited into her bed. None of that mattered now. All that was important was this moment. He grabbed a condom, tore it open and sheathed himself, then looked back to the woman waiting for him.

She was like a damned nymph, straight out of one of the fantasy games his company designed. Like one of her drawings—blond curls rumpled, blue eyes heated and languid all at once, curvy body lush and waiting for him.

"Now, Mike. I need you inside me, now."

"Yes, now." He pushed deep into her heat with one long stroke. Her body bowed beneath him, her legs hooked around his waist, pulling him tighter, deeper. He stared into her eyes, eyes that held what seemed to him the mysteries of the universe, and watching her, took what she offered. He rocked his body into hers, over and over, setting a breathtaking rhythm that she raced to meet.

Again and again, they parted and came together, each of them driving the other higher, faster. He heard her ragged breathing, felt the frantic slide and scratch of her nails at his back. The race for completion was all. They looked into each other's eyes, fierce now, impatient for what they knew was coming.

"Mike," she cried, gasping. "Oh, Mike!"

She grabbed his shoulders and held on as wave after wave of sensation crashed through her body, making her tremble and shudder violently in his arms.

He watched her eyes flash with satisfaction only seconds before his own body splintered and jolted into a wild pleasure that left him feeling jagged and shaken. Locked together, the two of them slid over the edge, riding the thunder and crash of completion. And willingly, Mike tumbled into the dark, locked in the arms of the one woman he couldn't have.

Three

Dawn crept into the room and stretched out long, golden fingers across the bed where Jenny lay beside Mike. For more than a year, she'd thought about him, wished things had been different, wanted him. And now he was here, sleeping in her bed, and she knew that as the sun rose, their time together was running out.

Nothing had changed between them. Not fundamentally. They hadn't settled the issues that had separated them for so long before falling into bed—they'd simply ignored them in favor of the desire arcing in the room like summer lightning. Basically, they'd taken a long time-out. She smiled to herself at the thought.

Turning her head on the pillow, she studied Mike, using the moment to really look at him while he was completely unaware. He didn't look young and innocent in his sleep, she thought. He looked sexy. Dangerous. Like the hard man he was. And yet... She curled her fingers into her palm to keep from reaching out, stroking his beard-shadowed jaw.

Jenny's heart took a slow tumble. Pitiful, she told herself with a heavy, inward sigh. How could she feel so much for a man who thought of her as a thief and worse? And why did she *care* what he thought about her?

"You're thinking too loud." He opened his eyes and stared at her.

"A lot to think about," she said just as quietly.

"I suppose," he agreed, one corner of his mouth lifting into a seductive smile. "But we don't have to think about it right this minute, do we?"

Under the blanket, Mike reached for her and slid one hand along her curves. Jenny held her breath as his hand glided up from her hip, along her ribs to cup her breast. She sighed when his thumb brushed across her nipple. No, they didn't have to think. Didn't have to let this night end just yet. The sun was coming up and soon enough, they'd have to face the real world again. The world where the two of them stood on opposite sides of a wall Jenny had believed would never be breached.

But for now...

"No," she said, moving into him, "there's no rush to start thinking."

He kissed her and as she fell into the swirl of sensations, Jenny put everything else out of her mind.

An hour later, though, she knew it was over. Even with his weight pressing her into the mattress, even with his body deep inside hers, she felt Mike pulling away from her. As physically close as they were at that moment, there was a distance between them that lovemaking couldn't bridge. All this time with him had actually managed to do was enforce the lines separating them. To make things worse, now it would be even harder to work with him over the coming months.

He rolled to the side and went up on one elbow. Shooting a quick glance at the window and the rays of sunlight peeking through, he shifted his gaze back to her and said, "I should go."

"Yeah." Jenny looked at him and sketched this view of him into her memory. Hair mussed, a shadow of whiskers and that amazing mouth of his quirked into a rueful smile. If she'd had any sense at all, instead of trying to build a memory, she would have been attempting to put this time with Mike out of her mind completely.

She wasn't sure where they would be going from here, but she knew that whatever connection they'd found, however briefly, was gone. Over.

"Look," he said, gently pushing her hair back from her face, "last night was—"

"A mistake, I know," she finished for him, since it was easier to say it than to hear it.

He frowned, rolled off the bed and grabbed his clothes, pulling them on while he talked. "Can't really call it a mistake since it was something we both wanted."

How did he do that? she wondered. He was right there, within reach, and yet he'd pulled so far away that he might as well have been in a different city. A cold ball of regret dropped into the pit of her stomach.

"Last night didn't change anything, Jenny."

She nearly sighed because she knew exactly where this conversation was headed. "I know, you don't trust me."

"You lied to me the first night I met you."

"I didn't lie," she argued tiredly. God, she hated having to defend herself over and over to a man who refused to see past his own suspicions. How could he sleep with her, make love with her and not have the slightest clue who she really was? "Since I've worked for Celtic Knot, haven't I done a good job? Have I ever let anyone down? Doesn't that count for something?"

"Yeah, it does," he said shortly. "You know it does. But it can't change the past." His features tightened and his mouth thinned into one grim line as he held up one hand for peace before she could respond.

"Let's not," he said. "You have done good work for us, Jenny. That's why we've got a problem now. You're the logical choice to do the work on the River Haunt hotel, but if we have to stay on the project together it's going to be more difficult than it has to be."

Shaking her head, she only stared at him. Difficult? Like going into the office every day and feeling him watching her warily? Like knowing that he was waiting for her to screw up? To prove that she was exactly the liar and cheat he took her for?

She pushed off the bed and quickly snatched her robe off the end of the bed. They weren't going to argue about the past, fine. But she was more than ready to fight for the present and her own future. And damned if she'd do it naked. Slipping the robe on, she belted it tightly, then shook her hair back and turned to face the man who continued to haunt her. "It's not a problem for me, Mike. I'm going to do a hell of a good job on that hotel. And it doesn't have to be difficult if you'll just trust me to do what I'm best at."

For a second she thought he might argue that point, but instead, he blew out a breath and shoved one hand through his hair. "All right. We do the hotel. We do the job. Then we're done."

Eager, wasn't he, to push her aside and keep her there? But even he had to realize that he'd said pretty much the same thing about being done with her more than a year before. And yet, here they were, facing each other across yet another rumpled bed.

Still, it's what she wanted, Jenny reminded herself. A chance to prove herself on the hotel project without being at war with Mike, because it really would make things harder. So why, she wondered, did she suddenly feel so terrible now that he was offering her just that? She scrubbed her hands up and down her arms as if to chase away the bone-deep chill crawling through her, but it didn't help.

"We keep…this," he said, waving one hand at the disheveled quilt and the still-warm sheets, "between us and do what we have to do."

Another secret, then, Jenny thought. But probably better that the people at work didn't know what was going on between them. Since even *she* wasn't sure what exactly it was they shared, beyond the burn and desire.

Nodding, she asked, "Do we shake hands on it?"

For the first time that morning his lips curved in a half smile. "I think we can do better than that."

He walked up to her, cupped her face between his palms and bent his head for a kiss. His mouth was firm, soft and left hers all too quickly. She really was an idiot, Jenny thought as her insides jumped and her heart galloped. The kiss meant nothing. *She* meant nothing to him and oh, boy, was that a hard thing to acknowledge. But she knew it was only hunger that burned between them, nothing more. Yet she looked into his eyes and found herself wishing things were different. Wishing for—

"I'll see you at the office?"

"Yeah," she said abruptly, cutting off her own thoughts before they could lead her down completely ridiculous paths. "I'll be there."

"All right, then." He turned away to grab his jacket off the floor. Shrugging it on, he looked back at her and said, "In honor of this new cooperation between us, I'd like you to go to Laughlin with me in a week or so. Check out the new hotel. I want to walk the property, get a feel for it before we start the renovations."

"Good." She forced a smile that she hoped looked more convincing than it felt. "It would be good for me to get an on-site idea for the placement of the murals."

"Okay." He tugged the jacket into place. "We'll go out a week from Monday. Figure to stay at least overnight. I'll have Linda make reservations at the River Lodge."

Her stomach jittered. Laughable really, because what virtue was she suddenly so worried about? But the two of them were practically combustible, so was it really wise to invite more temptation? "Overnight?"

He shrugged. "We'll take the company jet into Vegas, and drive into Laughlin from there. I want enough time to explore the place. Staying over is the only solution."

"Right." Overnight. Did that mean they'd be sharing a bed again? Was he expecting that? Well, if so, he was doomed to disappointment. Jenny wasn't going to let this spiral into an affair that would leave her broken and miserable when it ended. Better to end it now. And much better to let him know just where she stood on this before they went any further.

"I won't be sleeping with you again."

One dark eyebrow winged up. "I didn't say you would be."

"Just saying," she went on, shaking her head, "I'm not interested in an affair and I'm not going to keep sleeping with my boss."

A dark scowl marred his face briefly. "This wasn't about boss and employee. It never was."

She shivered under his steady stare, but lifted her chin to ask, "Then what was it about, Mike?"

"Need," he said simply, biting the single word off as if it tasted bitter.

There it was. Plain and simple. He didn't care about her, Jenny told herself. Probably didn't much like her. He certainly didn't trust her. She hated to admit that he was right about this, but she knew that hunger had drawn them together and then that same vicious desire had pulled them back in when they'd both believed it was done between them.

So no more. Of anything. They would have to work together for the next few months and sex—especially *great* sex—just complicated everything.

Over the next few days, Jenny almost convinced herself that nothing had happened between Mike and her. She spent her days concentrating on the art ideas for the new hotel. Using the photos and 360-degree videos provided by the real estate company, Jenny laid out her plans for the work to be done. But she couldn't really be sure of anything until she saw the place firsthand.

"Have you got the sketches for 'The Wild Hunt' done yet?"

She glanced up from her computer screen to look at Dave Cooper, the new head of graphic design. When her old supervisor, Joe, had left to take a job with one of the big Hollywood studios, they'd all missed him. But Dave had slid right into the position as if he'd always been there.

"You'll have them by tomorrow," she said. The next game they were working on was already taking shape and so far, Jenny loved doing the art for it. A wild hunt, complete with faery warriors, pookas and the supernatural beings that hunted them. No doubt, it would be another winner for Celtic Knot and she really enjoyed being a part of it.

"I think you'll like them." She'd been refining her sketches for the past few nights, polishing them so no one could say she'd neglected this project in favor of the art for the new hotel.

Dave grinned, eased one hip against the edge of her desk and pushed his glasses higher up the bridge of his nose. In his late thirties, he looked like a typical computer geek—tall, thin, with big brown eyes behind thick, black-rimmed glasses. He had a generous smile and a puppylike enthusiasm for the work. "I always like your stuff, Jen. I read your notes on the ideas you have for the drawings and I think they'll be great."

He was so nice, Jenny thought. It was a damn shame that all she felt for him was friendship. Life would have been much easier if only she'd been attracted to someone like Dave.

"Thanks." She smiled at him. "I'm glad you stopped by. There's something else I'd like to run past you."

"Yeah? What's up?"

"You know in 'The Wild Hunt,' there's the magical wolf terrorizing the village?"

"Yeah." Joe grinned wider and nodded his head eagerly. "Early renderings are awesome. Eric Santos worked it so that when the wolf transforms into a Black Knight, he retains the teeth and the yellow eyes. Truly excellent."

Eric did great work. He had an eye for detail that skipped most artists as they usually looked at the big picture and left the so-called inconsequential bits for the interns to fill in or expand on. Eric didn't work like that, though, and neither did Jenny, so she had a lot of respect for him.

"Sounds really great," she said, meaning it. "Can't wait to see it. But what I wanted to ask you about is, I've got this idea for another hero in the game program."

He frowned a little, clearly puzzled. "Another hero? We've already got Finn MacCool as the hero. He's the ancient Irish warrior. What're you thinking?"

Actually, she'd done a lot of thinking in the past few days. Trying to keep her mind busy and off Mike Ryan, Jenny had indulged herself with searching out Irish myths and playing with possible story lines. She'd even turned a few sketches into an abbreviated storyboard to pitch to Sean and Mike at some point. But her idea for "The Wild Hunt" was just a little something extra and if she ran it by Dave first, he'd let her know if it merited being presented to the Ryans.

"I was thinking that even a legendary hero like Finn MacCool could use a little help."

"Okay." Dave pushed his glasses up higher as they slid down his nose. "What've you got?"

"I was thinking it might be a nice twist to have a Wise Woman in the mix."

"Wise Woman?"

"You know, it's what they called witches back in the day."

He laughed. "Really? Interesting. Okay. Tell me."

Encouraged by the way he was giving her his complete concentration, Jenny started talking. Reaching into her top desk drawer, she pulled out a few sketches she'd made the night before. Handing them to Dave, she talked while he looked through them.

"She can live in the village. Almost like an Easter egg surprise, she wouldn't be activated unless the gamer hit a certain point on the quest."

Jenny paused, waited and was rewarded when Dave said, "Keep going."

"Okay." Tapping one finger on a storyboard of "The Wild Hunt," she said, "Here, in the timeline of the story, Finn finds a sword in a cave at the base of the cliffs. The gamer has to collect twelve rune clues to free the sword."

"Yeah…"

"Well, I was thinking, what if we laid down fifteen rune clues? Twelve to free the sword and allow the gamer to take Finn into combat with the wizard. *But*, if he finds all fifteen, then he unlocks the Wise Woman. She could help Finn defeat the forest demons and—"

"Be a love interest that maybe we could carry over into the sequel," Dave finished for her, studying the sketches of the witch. "That's excellent, Jenny. It adds another layer and rewards the gamer for collecting all of the runes." Nodding to himself, he added, "Game rules say twelve unlocks the sword, fifteen unlocks magic." He laughed to himself again and kept nodding. "Yeah, that'd be great. We make three of the runes really difficult to find so that players have to work for it if they want the extra. Most will just go for twelve and the sword, but the hard-core gamer will want to go for the magic. I like it." He lifted his gaze to Jenny's and added, "You should take this to the Ryans. Get their okay. They'll love it."

"Um…" she said, pleasure sliding away at the thought of talking to the Ryan brothers together. Sean would be okay. He was nice, reasonable and he liked her. Mike on the other hand… "Why don't you do it? You're the head of my department."

He looked surprised. "It's your idea, Jenny, and it's a great one."

"Yeah, but—"

"Don't be dumb," he said and dropped the sketches onto her desk. "Sean's in Mike's office. You can pitch it to both of them at the same time. The sooner you get this to them the better. Programmers will need more time to set up the extra layers."

"I know, but—"

Dave chuckled a little. "Since when are you shy? Come on, take your idea to the bosses, impress the hell out of 'em."

Still shaking his head, he wandered off to check on a couple of the other artists. Jenny watched him go, then dropped her gaze to the Wise Woman sketches. It *was* a good idea, damn it. And if she and Mike weren't…she didn't know what they were exactly, but if they weren't in such a weird space, she'd have no trouble at all taking her ideas to the Ryan brothers. They were always open to the employees coming to them with suggestions.

She was the head artist now, so she shouldn't be wary of facing her bosses. This was her job, and hadn't she made a point out of telling Mike that nothing was going to stop her from doing her job?

Nodding to herself, she gathered up her sketches and headed out of the office.

* * *

Mike and Sean were going over the figures sent by the collectibles company. "The licensing fee is good, but did you take a look at their latest batch of figurines based on that kids' movie?"

"Yeah," Sean said with a wince. "I admit, they're not great."

Mike snorted. "'Not great' covers a lot of territory. This can be narrowed down to crappy."

"Okay, yeah." Sean tossed the pictures back on his brother's desk. "If they couldn't get the talking frog and the Princess Knight right…"

"Exactly," Mike agreed. "Those are easy. What'll they do to our banshees, warlocks and Irish warriors?" Shaking his head, he continued, "Brady and I both went along with this idea of yours, Sean. But if this is what the collectibles are going to look like, I don't know if it's a good thing."

"True." Sean crossed his legs, propping one ankle on his knee. "There are other companies we could try."

"Is it worth it?"

"I think so," Sean countered. "If we get into the collectibles market, it's going to push our name recognition even higher and affect game sales. We could pull in gamers who haven't tried us yet."

Mike frowned and tapped his fingertips against the desk. It was hard to keep his mind on business. Even now, while his brother continued to talk about his plan, Mike's mind drifted to the woman working on the floor above him.

Three days since his night with Jenny and he'd hardly been able to shake thoughts of her for five minutes at a stretch. He'd convinced himself that spending the night with her had been a wise choice. A way to not only ease the ache for her but a chance to push away the memories of that one night in Phoenix.

Well, that had worked, but now it was memories of a night in Long Beach that tormented him. Rather than getting her out of his mind, that night had only entrenched her there.

"Are you listening to me?" Sean demanded.

"What?" Mike scowled and shot his brother a hard look. "Yeah. Sure."

"Uh-huh." Sean smirked at him. "What did I just say?"

"Collectibles. Gamers. Blah, blah. Pretty much what you've been saying for months."

"Right. So what's going on with you?"

"Nothing," Mike said, picking up a pen and twirling it idly between his fingers. "I'm busy."

"Yeah," Sean said, "me, too. So what's going on?"

"Who're you all of a sudden?" Mike asked. "Mom?"

"Hah. If I was Mom I'd get an answer to my question."

True. Peggy Ryan was tough and had a way of getting her family to confess all. Which, Mike reminded himself, wasn't always a good thing. She'd once pried truths out of her husband that had changed the way Mike felt about his father forever. It was the day that Mike learned how much damage liars and cheats could do.

And that thought steeled his spine and firmed his resolve to get past whatever it was he was feeling for Jenny. Liars had no place in his life and damned if he'd forget that.

As if his thoughts had conjured her, a perfunctory knock on the open door announced her presence. Mike looked at her, his gaze locking with hers, and he felt a fast jolt of awareness tangled up with a bone-deep need that just never seemed to drain away. "What is it?"

She blinked at the brusque tone, then deliberately looked away from him to Sean. "I had an idea I wanted to run past you. For 'The Wild Hunt.'"

Sean glanced at Mike, then shrugged and said, "Sure, Jenny. Come on in."

He waved her into a chair and she sat, still avoiding looking at Mike directly. "I was talking with Dave, showed him a few sketches, and he said I should bring it to you guys."

Mike watched her lips move, heard her voice, but couldn't concentrate on what she was saying as she explained her idea for a new character to drop into "The Wild Hunt." Instead, his brain insisted on dredging up images from the other night. How the hell could he focus on work with rich, sexual memories flooding his brain and torturing his body?

"Those are great," Sean was saying. He leaned close to Jenny to look at the sketch she held and a flash of irritation shook Mike in response.

Why the hell did Sean have to practically drape himself over Jenny's shoulder to get a look at her sketch pad?

"Let me see," he said abruptly, breaking up what looked to him like a too-cozy scene.

Sean passed the drawings over and said, "I think she's onto something. I like the idea of a powerful woman coming to the aid of the beleaguered hero." He grinned. "Might get more female players out of it, too."

Nodding, Mike scanned the drawings and once again was forced to admit just how talented Jenny Marshall really was. The sketches weren't complete, more of a bare-bones idea for a new character, but even at that stage, he could see the beauty that would pop through when it was finished. The witch was tall, powerful, magical, a perfect addition to the game cast.

He slanted a look at Jenny and found her watching him, waiting for whatever he was going to say. And in her eyes, he saw resignation, as if she was expecting him to shoot down her ideas. Well, hell, he might have some issues with her, but he wasn't an idiot.

"This is good work."

"Wow, high praise," Sean muttered and earned a quick, grateful grin from Jenny.

Mike ignored a new flash of irritation and kept talking. "I'll keep the high praise for when I see the fleshed-out ideas. But for now, I agree. It's a good addition to the game."

A slow, pleased smile curved Jenny's mouth and everything in Mike warmed, softened. The effect this woman had on him was dangerous. And it didn't seem to be dissipating any.

"Thank you," she said simply. Her eyes shone with a deeper gratitude that only Mike was aware of. It made him feel like a damn bully to know that she had fully expected him to shoot down her ideas just because they were hers.

He handed the sketches back and turned to his brother. "What do you think? Can we come up with a new story line and get it to the writers by the weekend?"

"Probably," Sean said, then shrugged. "But what's the rush?"

Mike slanted a look at Jenny. "Because Jenny and I are headed to Laughlin to check out the new hotel. We're leaving on Monday. Be gone a couple days."

She shifted a little uneasily in her chair and Mike

caught the motion. He could only hope Sean hadn't. Sometimes, Mike's little brother saw too damn much.

"Well, then," Sean said and stood up. "I'll talk to the writers, get them to amend the script. Meanwhile," he added, "if you could finish out those sketches, that'd be great, Jenny."

"I can have them to you in an hour," she said, rising and heading to the door.

"Great. You want to start on the storyboard changes now, Sean?"

"Should we call Brady before making a final decision?"

Mike thought about it, then scrubbed one hand across the back of his neck. "No. We'll tell him about it at our next conference call, but he'll be on board."

"Okay." Sean headed out. "I'll get the stuff together."

"Be right there," Mike called after him. When they were alone, he stood up and asked, "Leaving Monday work for you?"

"Oh," Jenny said, giving a quick look over her shoulder as if to make sure the hallway behind her was empty. "So you *are* going to ask me? I thought you were just handing out a royal decree."

Mike grimaced and stuffed his hands into his pants pockets. "We talked about going to the hotel."

"Yeah, but you didn't give me a specific date," she countered. "And I was supposed to have dinner with my uncle on Monday."

Everything in Mike fisted at the reminder of Hank Snyder, her uncle and the owner of Snyder Arts.

"You don't have to make that face," she told him. "You might not like my uncle," Jenny added, "but I love him. He's my family."

"That's the problem, isn't it?"

"For you, yes."

A couple of people walked down the hall, their voices raised in argument.

"Zombies have to die when you cut their heads off."

"In real life, not in the gaming world, hello?"

"We have to at least try to be realistic, don't we?"

"You want realism, then our zombies have to eat brains, not just bite people…"

Their voices faded as they went into the break room and shut the door after them. A moment later, Jenny chuckled. "Zombies in real life." She looked up at Mike, the smile still curving her mouth. "We have weird lives."

All he could see was that smile and after a second or two, he returned it. "Yeah, I guess we do. So. Monday?"

"I'll be ready," she said, all trace of amusement disappearing. "Should I meet you here?"

He shook his head. "I'll pick you up at nine. We'll take the company jet to Vegas."

"Okay." She took a breath, blew it out. "Now, I'd better go see about finishing the images of my Wise Woman."

Mike crossed the room and propped one shoulder against the doorjamb. Watching her go, he wondered if, when all this was done, seeing her walk away from him would be his clearest memory.

Four

"I'll only be gone overnight, Uncle Hank."

"With *him*," Hank Snyder muttered under his breath.

Jenny sighed and let her head fall back. It was Monday morning; Mike would be here in a few minutes and she still had to finish packing. But as her uncle went on a long-winded rant, she realized having to listen to this was her own fault.

She never should have confessed to her uncle what Mike had accused her of a year ago. But in her defense, she had really been upset, and Hank had dropped by her apartment just when she was in the middle of a good rant. So instead of shutting up, she'd spewed everything at the feet of the man who'd raised her.

Naturally, his first instinct had been to go to Celtic Knot and punch Mike Ryan in the mouth. Thankfully, she'd talked him down from that. But he hadn't forgiven and he hadn't forgotten. In fact, Hank had tried to talk her out of going to work for the Ryan brothers on the principle that she should simply stay the hell away from Mike altogether. But Jenny had refused, then and now, to let Mike Ryan's presence dictate how she ran her life and career.

"He is my boss," she finally said.

"Doesn't have to be," Hank told her, and Jenny's hand fisted around her phone. "You could come to work for me. You know that."

Snyder Arts was a small company with an excellent arts program. The program itself simplified digital and graphic arts design and implementation. They sold retail and to companies looking to refine their own graphic art departments. Which is why Hank had tried to make a deal with Celtic Knot in the first place. He'd thought—and *rightly*, Jenny acknowledged—that his program would streamline the gaming company's art and design division.

And since Jenny now knew *both* companies well, she understood that if Mike weren't so hardheaded, even he would have to admit that her uncle's program would make the work easier for his own artists. But Mike being Mike, he would never let himself see that. Especially since he believed that Hank had tried to use Jenny to worm a contract out of Mike.

She sighed and leaned against the bathroom door. "I do know that, Uncle Hank. And I appreciate it. Really. But I'm not interested in R & D or in sales and marketing. I'm an artist and I'm good at what I do."

"You're the best, honey," he said on a belabored sigh. "I just don't like you being upset is all. And I really don't like you having to deal with a man who thinks so little of you."

"It doesn't matter what Mike thinks of me personally," she said, though in her head she was chanting, *Liar, liar, pants on fire.* "I like my job. And this trip to Laughlin will be fast and all business. I want to scope out the hotel in person so I can start planning the murals."

"Never could argue with you once you had your mind set on something, could I?"

Jenny smiled. "Nope."

"Fine, fine. You just be careful and you let me know when you're home safe."

"I will." Then Jenny listened as her uncle talked about what was happening at Snyder Arts. His R & D department was coming up with some interesting things. Jenny knew how important his company was to him. Until she had come into his life and he had taken over as her guardian, that company had been his entire world.

But the main point in all this was Hank didn't need a deal with Celtic Knot to make Snyder Arts profitable. Their bottom line was very comfortable. Okay, not billionaire comfy, but still. It was laughable that Hank would have needed her to coax Mike into some kind of deal even if it hadn't been insulting on the face of it. Snyder Arts didn't need Celtic Knot and Mike had to know that, in some part of himself. He was just so down-to-the-marrow suspicious and hard, he'd never admit it.

While Hank talked, she smiled to herself and quickly packed away her hair products and makeup, zipping them into a small purple bag. She walked into the bedroom, tucked the bag into her suitcase and sat on the edge of the bed.

Now she was packed and ready to go. Well, as ready

as she could be. Two days alone with Mike would be either a misery or wonderful—and that would turn into misery later. The man wanted her, that was plain enough. But he didn't want to want her and she had no idea how to get past that. Or even if she should try.

Jenny had spent a lifetime knowing that she wasn't wanted. Heck, her own parents had walked away from her and never looked back. She was twelve when they decided they didn't really want the burden of a child and were bored with being parents. They'd dropped her off with Hank, her mother's older brother.

Hank was a widower who had buried himself in his company at his wife's death. Barely home back then, he'd had to shift his entire life around to accommodate Jenny. And she'd known it. She'd tried to be as invisible as possible so that he, too, wouldn't decide to walk away.

Even as a kid, Jenny had known that Hank didn't really *want* her. Taking her in had simply been the right thing to do. But Hank had always been kind and supportive, and she was still grateful to him for so much.

"You're not listening," Hank said with a short laugh.

Caught, she said, "I'm sorry, Uncle Hank. My mind wandered."

"That's fine. I know you're getting ready to leave."

True. Mike would be arriving any minute. Well, there went the knots in her stomach, tightening viciously enough that it was hard to breathe.

"I'll just remind you to be careful."

"I will, promise." Jenny glanced out the window, saw Mike's car pulling up and said, "I've really gotta go."

Her uncle hung up, still muttering direly. Jenny tucked her phone into her pocket, zipped her suitcase closed and told herself to relax. Not that she was listening, but she had to try. Outside, Mike stepped out of his car, looked at her apartment and for just a second, Jenny felt as if he were looking directly into her eyes. That was stupid of course, but it didn't change the zip of heat that raced through her.

This was probably a mistake. Two days. Alone. With Mike Ryan.

No way this was going to end well.

Traveling with a gazillionaire was eye-opening.

Even at the small airport in Long Beach, people practically snapped to attention for Mike Ryan. Baggage handlers hurried to stow the overnight bags they both carried, then the pilot stepped out onto the stairway to welcome them aboard personally.

Once they'd boarded the private jet, Jenny curled up in a buttery-soft leather seat and sipped at the fresh coffee served by a friendly attendant. Mike concentrated on work, staring so hard at the screen of his tablet, Jenny was almost surprised he didn't burn a hole through it. But left to herself, she watched the clouds and enjoyed the all-too-short flight.

In less than an hour, they were landing in Las Vegas. There again, people scrambled to make Mike's life easier, smoother. A rental car was waiting for them and after forty minutes on a nearly empty highway flanked on either side by wide sweeps of desert, they were in Laughlin, Nevada.

Laughlin was sort of the more casual, fun, younger sister of Las Vegas. There were plenty of casino hotels, but there was also the Colorado River. In the summer, the town was booming with water-skiers and boaters and everyone looking for a good time on the water. Then the hot desert nights featured riverside dining or visits to the casinos where top-name acts performed on glittery stages.

Jenny had been there before, though the last time had been five years ago for a bachelorette party. Remembering, she smiled. That party was the reason she'd had condoms in her bedside drawer a week ago when Mike had shown up at her apartment. As a party favor, the condoms had seemed silly at the time, but now, Jenny could appreciate the gesture because without them, she wouldn't have had that spectacular night.

The town had grown a lot in five years. There were new casinos springing up everywhere along with housing developments and shopping centers just out of sight of the big hotels.

In late January, the weather was cool and the river ran high and fast. Jenny stood on the shore and looked upstream toward the heart of the city where big hotels lined the Riverwalk—a wooden boardwalk that stretched the length of hotel row. At night, she knew, there were old-fashioned streetlights sending out a golden glow along the walk. There were restaurants and bars, where a couple could sit and talk and look out over the water.

The Ryans had made a good choice in building their hotel here. All in all, Jenny told herself, if she had a choice, she would come to Laughlin instead of Vegas. It was smaller, friendlier and offered a variety of things to do.

She shrugged deeper into her navy blue jacket as a hard, cold wind carrying the sharp tang of sage blew in off the desert. There were clouds on the horizon promising a storm, but for the moment, the sky was a bright blue and all around her, trees dipped and swayed in the wind. Jenny walked out onto the boat dock and watched as the river churned and sloshed below her.

"It's a good spot."

She turned her head into the wind to look back at the shore. Mike was headed her way, hands tucked into the pockets of his black leather jacket.

Nodding, Jenny shifted her gaze to the river again. "I was just thinking that. There are so many trees on the grounds, you could almost forget you're in the desert."

"Yeah, now," he said, a chuckle in his voice as he came closer. "Wait until summer."

She smiled. Temperatures in the desert regularly topped out at one hundred twenty and more during the summer. But as the locals liked to say, *It's a dry heat.* "Agreed. But you can go in the river to cool off."

"Or the hotel pool," he said as he joined her at the edge of the dock.

"True."

Upstream, there were flat-bottom boats, owned by the hotels, taking tourists for river rides. The windows and gold trim on the hotels winked brightly in the sunlight. But here, standing in the shadows of the nest of trees edging the river, it was as if they were alone.

"I wonder why the previous owners couldn't make the hotel work," she mused aloud. "It's a great spot. Wonderful views, plenty of trees, a gorgeous pool—"

"No gambling."

She looked at him. "What?"

"The hotel." Mike squinted into the sun. "The old owner didn't approve of gambling so the hotel didn't offer it." He shrugged. "A hotel with no casino in a gambling town isn't going to survive. Plus, he didn't have smoking rooms, either."

"That's important?"

"Again, a gambling town. People come here looking to relax, throw a little money down a rat hole…" He looked at her. "They're not interested in being snubbed because they smoke. Or if they can't find a slot machine anywhere on the premises."

"Good points." He was always thinking and she shouldn't have been surprised to know that he'd done his homework on the previous owner's failures and come to his own conclusions. Mike Ryan always had a plan. "So, you'll have gambling?"

He gave her a fast grin. "Not a regular casino, no. But we'll have some custom-made slot machines if people are interested. Based on the game, of course."

"Of course." She smiled and looked up at him. He was so tall, so broad shouldered. His dark hair ruffled in the wind and his blue eyes were narrowed on the distant view, as if he was staring off into a future that lay waiting for him to conquer it.

Oh, she really had to stop.

"Still," Mike said, grabbing her attention again, "the River Haunt isn't going to be your standard hotel. It's being designed to appeal to gamers—not gamblers."

"Gamblers like games, too."

"Yeah," Mike said. "But they're more interested in risking their money for the chance of a big reward. A gamer wants to beat his time, beat the game." He turned and looked back up the rise to the hotel that now belonged to Celtic Knot. "The people who come here are going to be looking for the experience. The opportunity to pretend they're a part of the game they love. Gambling doesn't have anything to do with that."

"But you'll have a few slot machines just in case."

He winked at her. "Doesn't hurt to cover all bases."

Pleasure rushed through Jenny at that friendly wink.

She liked this. They were talking. About important things, and he hadn't taken a single shot at her yet. No insults, no disapproval. Maybe it was being away from their everyday routine, but whatever the reason, she was enjoying it. And maybe, she thought, these two days with Mike wouldn't be as hard as she'd thought they would be.

"I'm guessing you'll have smoking rooms, too, then," she said with a smile.

"Absolutely," he said. "I'm not going to cut anyone out of coming to the hotel." He shook his hair back when the wind tossed it across his forehead. "It's ridiculous for any business owner to discriminate against possible customers."

"Agreed," she said. Half turning, she looked back at the hotel sitting at the top of a low rise.

It was old, but sturdy. Paint that had once been a deep brick red had faded in the sun until it looked almost pink. The building sprawled across the property but Jenny knew that compared to the rich new hotels farther downriver this place was small. Only a hundred and fifty rooms, the soon-to-be River Haunt hotel would be exclusive and that would appeal to the gamers who would flock here.

There was a wide porch that swept along the front of the building, and floor-to-ceiling windows provided a great view of the river and the purple smudge of mountains in the distance. The now pink paint was peeling and the plain boxlike structure wasn't exactly appealing, but she knew that Mike would be changing it all up. The rehab wouldn't go fast, but she could imagine it all as it would be in a few months.

Like the setting of the "River Haunt" game, the main building would be made to look like a weathered, deserted cabin. A cabin where ghouls, ghosts, zombies and other assorted supernatural beings assembled and tormented the gamers who fought to defeat Donn, Lord of the Dead.

The guests at the River Haunt hotel would be treated to rooms and suites decked out with top-of-the-line gaming systems, flat-screen TVs and enough gaming tokens and symbols to make them feel as though they were a part of their favorite game. The latest Celtic Knot hotel was going to be huge.

"It'll be a lot of work," Jenny said thoughtfully.

"It will."

She turned and flashed him a quick smile. "But it's gonna be great."

"Damn straight."

His gaze locked with hers and for one bright, amazing moment, Jenny felt like they were a team. In this together. And in that impossibly fast heartbeat of time, she really wished it were true.

They were making the most of their two days in Nevada.

Mike spent hours with his contractor, Jacob Schmitt, going over the plans for the River Haunt. The two of them walked the hotel, checking out the rooms and talking to the skeleton staff who remained on-site.

Mike appreciated good work and loyalty, so when he was given the opportunity to keep on some of the hotel employees, he did. He wasn't a soft touch, though, so in interviews with the hotel manager, and the heads of the other departments, he'd quickly weeded out the people who were simply dead weight.

Maybe the previous owner's standards had been lax,

but Mike had no intention of paying people to do nothing. But he was also ready to pay top money for the right kind of employee. Which was why he'd fired the previous manager and promoted that man's assistant, Teresa Graves.

Teresa was a middle-aged woman with a no-nonsense attitude and an unerring ability to cut through the bull and get the best out of the people who worked for her. With his new manager's help, Mike wanted to keep the skeleton crew in place during the transition. He didn't want the hotel sitting empty and deserted while it was being rehabbed. It seemed like too much of an invitation to vandals and or thieves.

Having people there was important enough that he was offering bonuses to the workers who were willing to actually *live* in the hotel so that someone besides the security people he'd hired were around 24/7. With a working kitchen, a pool and plenty of guest rooms to choose from, it was no hardship for those who chose to stay. Plus, they were paid enough that they didn't have to look for another job while waiting for the hotel to reopen.

"I figure we'll do the pool last," Jacob said as they walked through the main lobby and out onto the sun-splashed deck. "Leave it as is so your people can use it while we work. And this way, with all the construction going on, we don't risk breaking up the new tiles you wanted in the pool surround."

Mike studied the architect's line drawings for a long moment.

"That's a good idea," he said finally. "Pool's going to be the last thing we need done anyway."

"Yeah, and these tiles we'll be laying in the deck and surround aren't something we want scratched up." Jacob yanked his battered blue ball cap with a faded Dodgers patch off his head and rubbed the wild scrub of gray hair that sprung up as if freed from prison. "Just like you wanted, the tiles actually look like rough wood—gives the feel of the forest floor."

Mike glanced at the man and smiled. "You know the 'River Haunt' game?"

"I should," the other man said. "My son plays the damn thing every chance he gets." Chuckling, he added, "I swear, I hear banshees wailing in my dreams."

"That's good to hear, too," Mike said, and gave the other man a friendly slap to the shoulder.

"I'll bet." Jacob Schmitt turned slowly to take a look around the property. "This is a perfect spot for what you're wanting. My opinion, the last owner didn't make enough of what he had. But his loss—your gain."

"That's what I think, too."

"You know, my son's already nagging at me to bring him to the hotel for a long weekend."

Mike followed the other man's gaze and realized that he was anxious to get this hotel up and running, too. He couldn't wait to see how it all came out. "Tell you what," Mike said. "You bring the job in on time and on budget, you and your family can stay a week, on us."

The older man's bushy gray brows shot high on his forehead as he gave a wide smile. "My son will think I'm a god."

Mike laughed. "Anything I can do."

Eager now, Jacob pointed to the sketch of the pool area. "You can see this wall behind the pool will be a series of ledges, each of them planted with flowering plants that will trail down to the edge of the pool itself."

Mike listened as he looked at the ink drawings, bringing it all to life in his mind. He had a good imagination and used it to mentally change the plain, kidney-shaped pool into the fantasy spot he wanted.

He could almost see it. A waterfall would cascade at one end of the pool and behind that waterfall would be a swim-up bar where guests could be served as they hid behind a froth of water. There would be lounge chairs in deep forest green and tables that looked like the twisted limbs of ancient trees. The flowering vines Jacob described would be a curtain of green in the desert heat. It was a very good representation of the kind of scenery found in the "River Haunt" game.

Hell, Mike thought he could practically hear the groaning zombies approaching. He'd like to show the sketches to Jenny, get her opinion. After all, she was here to work, he reminded himself. But she was inside, scouting out the right places for the murals she would design and paint.

"I've expanded the dock," the contractor said, getting Mike's attention again, "so you'll have room for both of the boats you're planning for."

"That's good. We want to offer late-night cruises as part of the experience."

"It's pretty out here at night," the contractor said with a nod as he lifted his gaze to look around. "Far enough away from hotel row, you can see the stars like you never would in the city."

"Yeah?" It had been a long time since Mike had even taken the time to look up at a night sky. But it was part of the whole experience his guests would have. "What did you think of the idea for the animatronics?"

Jacob chuckled and tugged his hat back into place. "I

think it's gonna scare the hell out of your guests," he said. "But I suppose that's why they're coming here, isn't it?"

"It is." Mike nodded to himself and glanced toward the riverbank that stretched along the front of their property. Plenty of thick, high bushes and trees to hide the mechanics of the banshees and river specters who would be made to move in and out of the shadows as the gamers drifted by on the water. He could practically see how it would play out and he was anxious to get it all going.

"We're working with the engineers to make the housings for the creatures to move on as well as the shells they'll retreat to so they're protected from the elements," Jacob said.

"You can hide the housings well enough they won't be seen?"

"Absolutely."

It all sounded good. Hell, perfect. With any luck at all, the hotel would be finished and ready to welcome guests by summer. Hot desert nights, dark skies, perfect for scaring the hell out of people.

"I've got the best crew in Nevada," Jacob assured him. "We'll get it all done just the way you want it."

Nodding, Mike said, "I'll be making trips out to check on things, but Ms. Graves, the new manager, will be the point person on this. You go to her with any issues if you can't get hold of me. She'll make sure I'm kept up to date."

"I'll do that, and don't worry, it's going to be something special when it's done."

"Agreed," Mike told him, then turned back to the hotel. "Let's go through the kitchen work that needs doing. I want to hear about any potential problems."

"Well," Jacob said as he fell into step beside him,

"we've got a few of those, too. But nothing to be worried about."

Mike only half listened as they headed inside. He had researched every aspect of this rehab. He knew Jacob Schmitt would deliver good work done at a fair price. He knew Teresa Graves could be trusted to keep on top of the day-to-day issues that were bound to crop up. And he was sure that the security company he'd hired would protect his property.

Of course, the only thing he wasn't sure of in all this was Jenny. He hadn't seen her since the conversation on the dock hours ago. Probably best to keep a distance between them, but damned if he didn't want to go find her. Talk to her. Look at her.

And more.

Yeah, not going there.

"Right, Jacob. Let's get back to work."

Five

Jenny's imagination was in overdrive. She'd brought her ideas for murals with her and she'd spent the past two hours walking the halls and the big rooms on the main floor, plotting just where she'd put them.

The restaurant was perfect for a wide mural on the back wall. She would paint it as if there was a path leading from the room into the forest itself. Sort of a trompe l'oeil, giving the guests in the room the feeling that they could simply step into the painting. Of course, being gamers, they would know what lurked in that forest, she thought with a smile, so maybe they wouldn't want to follow the path.

On the opposite wall, there were tall windows, displaying the view of the tree-laden yard and the river beyond. Those she would surround with deep green vines, twining down the wall to pool on the floor.

She took a deep breath and simply sighed at the pleasure of having so many blank canvases just waiting to be turned into fantasies. Her hands actually itched to take hold of her brushes. God knew, she loved her job, but having the opportunity to paint rather than generating images on a computer was just…fun.

Grinning, she left the dining room and walked into the lobby. She had a great idea for the main entrance to the hotel and knew that it was only because she'd been here to see it in person that the thought had occurred to her. She wanted this painting to make a statement. To show the gamers and other guests that from the moment they walked into the hotel, they were stepping into another realm.

The lobby area was another big, gorgeous space that only needed some attention to really wake it up and make it special. And Jenny was just the artist to do it. There were a few crewmen in the room already, tearing out the old reception desk. It was white and sterile and too contemporary-looking for what the Ryans had in mind, so it had to go.

"Excuse me," she said and waited until one of the men turned to look at her to ask, "who do I speak to about the color of paint I want on this entry wall?"

"Oh, that'd be Jacob." A guy in his thirties with big brown eyes, a heavy mustache and deeply tanned skin smiled at her, touching off a dimple in one cheek. "I think he's in the kitchen with the boss."

"Okay, thanks." She started that way, but stopped when the man spoke again.

"You're the artist, right? Jenny?"

Jenny turned to face him. "That's right."

"Nice to meet you. I'm Rick."

He really was cute and that dimple was disarming. His jeans were worn and faded, and his white T-shirt strained over a build that was truly impressive. And Jenny was pretty sure Rick knew exactly how good he looked. There was something in his stance—as if he were posing for her admiration—and in the knowing gleam in his eyes that told Jenny he was used to women curling up at his feet and staring up at him adoringly.

Hard to blame them.

"Hi, Rick," she said. "Good to meet you, too. I'm going to be doing the murals for the new hotel. Well," she hedged, "not me all on my lonesome. It would take me ten years to do all of them myself.

"But I'm doing the designs and supervising the artists we'll bring in to finish the job."

He nodded as if he cared and she knew he didn't. Please. Were most of her gender really so easily manipulated by a gorgeous face and the appearance of interest in what they were saying?

"So what color do you want for that wall?" he asked.

She glanced at the wall in question. It was the first thing you saw when you walked into the hotel. Right now, it was cream colored, with sun stains from where framed paintings had once hung. But when Jenny was finished with it, it was going to be…mystical.

When she spoke, she wasn't really talking to Rick-With-Dimples. Instead, she was describing her vision to herself, sort of putting it out into the universe.

"Deep purple," she said, tipping her head to stare at the blank space as if she could see the wall changing color as she spoke. "I want it the color of twilight just before darkness falls. There will be stars, just barely appearing in the sky, with dark clouds streaming past a full moon, making them shine like silver." She sighed and continued, "There'll be a forest beneath the stars and moonlight threading through the trees. And in the shadows, there will be the hint of yellow eyes, red eyes, staring out at you, and you won't be sure if you see them or not.

"But the night will draw you in, make promises, and you'll dream about that forest and the eyes that follow you as you walk."

She fell silent and was still staring at the blank wall when she heard Rick say, "Damn, lady, you're a little spooky, you know that?"

She laughed, until Mike's voice came from right behind her.

"You have no idea."

Whipping around, she looked up into Mike's eyes and noticed the all-too-familiar flare of anger. Well, for heaven's sake, what had she done *now*?

"Don't you have work to do?" Jacob asked Rick and he immediately left, doing his best to look busy.

"Thanks for the tour, Jacob," Mike was saying. "We'll meet up here again tomorrow."

"I'll be here," the older man said, with a nod acknowledging Jenny. "You make a note on the paint colors you want where, miss, and I'll make sure the painters get the message."

"Thank you. I'll have them for you tomorrow, then."

"That's good." Jacob looked back at Mike. "The crew starts on the main floor in the morning. You and I can look at the upper floors and talk about what you want."

"See you then." Mike took Jenny's elbow and began steering her toward the front door.

She pulled free though, because A, she wasn't going

to be dragged around like a dog on a leash. And B, she needed her purse.

"Just wait a minute," she snapped and marched across the front room like a soldier striding across a battlefield. Snatching up her black leather bag, she slung it over her shoulder and stomped right back to Mike. "*Now* I'm ready."

He gritted his teeth. She could see the muscle in his jaw twitching and she almost enjoyed knowing she had the ability to irritate him so easily. Of course, she'd enjoy it even more if she knew what exactly she'd done to make him walk as if there were a steel spike between his shoulder blades.

Without waiting for him, Jenny walked out the front door, down the overgrown walk and stopped at the passenger door of the shiny red rental car to wait.

He looked at her over the roof of the car and demanded, "What the hell were you doing?"

"My *job*," she shot back, then threw the door open and slid inside.

He did the same, slammed the key home and fired the engine. Neither of them spoke again on the short drive to the hotel where they'd be spending the night.

When they got there, Mike turned the car over to the valet and Jenny was inside the hotel before he caught up to her. Again, he took hold of her elbow and pulled her to a stop.

"Will you quit doing that?" Her gaze shot from his hand on her arm up to his eyes.

"Quit walking away from me."

"Quit being a jerk and I'll quit walking away."

"You make me nuts," he grumbled.

"I think you were born that way," she said, "but Sean

seems perfectly reasonable, so it's probably not heredi-
tary."

All around them, tourists swarmed through the lobby
and into the casino. Bells, whistles and loud bursts of
laughter played backdrop to their hurried, angry whis-
pers.

"I'm not having this conversation here."

Jenny flinched at the cold, sharp edge of his voice.
"I'm not having it at all."

"Yeah you are. We'll talk about it upstairs. Your room
or mine?"

"Ha!" She laughed shortly. "Despite that charming
invitation, I think I'll pass."

"We talk privately," he said, lowering his voice until
it was a hush, "or we do it right here in the middle of
the damn hotel."

"Fine. Upstairs. My room because I want to be able
to tell you to leave."

He snorted, took her elbow in a grip firm enough she
couldn't shake him off and steered her to the bank of elevators. One of them opened instantly as soon as Mike
stabbed the call button. The two of them stepped into
the open car as soon as it emptied and were joined by a
half-dozen other people.

The elevator was crowded and the piped-in music was
straight out of the 1980s. Mirrors on the walls made it
seem as if there were fifty people crammed together, but
the only person Jenny really looked at was Mike. He was
at least a head taller than anyone else and in the mirror,
his gaze shifted to hers and held. The car stopped, people
got off, got on, and then they were moving again. Conversations rippled around them, but Jenny hardly heard
them. All she could focus on was the glint in Mike's

eyes and the grim slash of his mouth. Finally, though, they hit the eleventh floor. Jenny stepped off and Mike followed after.

The hallway was dimly lit and narrow, and with Mike right behind her, felt even tighter. She reached her door, slid the card key through the slot and opened it. Jenny'd left her drapes open, so afternoon sunlight swamped the room as she walked to the bed and tossed her purse down on it.

Mike closed the door and was walking toward her when she turned to face him.

"What the hell was that all about?"

"What was what about?" Jenny threw both hands high and then let them fall.

"You and the carpenter." Mike bit the words off. "When I walked into the lobby, you were flirting and he was drooling, so I ask again, what the hell was that about?"

Sincerely stunned, Jenny gaped at him for a second or two. "Flirting?" she repeated as anger bubbled and churned in the pit of her stomach. "I was talking about *paint*. About the mural I want on the wall in the lobby."

"Yeah, I heard the end of the performance." Mike cut her off with a wave of his hand. "Deep, breathy voice going all dreamy and soft. Hell, you had that carpenter standing there with his mouth open and his eyes bugging out."

"Dreamy? Soft?" Had she really sounded like that, she wondered, then shook her head to dismiss the question. Didn't matter if she had, Jenny thought. She hadn't been flirting, she'd been sort of lost in her own vision.

Mike inhaled sharply and said, "You sounded just like you did when you woke up in my arms."

Now it was her turn to drag a deep breath into her lungs. Reminding her of their most recent night together wasn't playing fair. "You're wrong."

He took a step closer, grabbed her upper arms and pulled her up against him. Jenny's heart leaped into a gallop and as he was holding her so tightly to him, she felt his heart raging in the same rhythm.

"I know what I heard," he said, staring down into her eyes. "What I saw."

She fought the natural impulse to wrap her arms around his waist and hold on. To go up on her toes and kiss him. To feel that rush of incredible sensations one more time. Instead, she reminded herself just how little he really thought of her. Of the fact that he didn't want her—it was only desire driving his reactions.

"I wasn't flirting," she told him. "But even if I had been, what business is that of yours? You're my boss, Mike, not my boyfriend."

"I am your boss," he agreed. "And I don't want you playing with the crew. I want them focused on the work, not you."

Stunned all over again, Jenny demanded, "Can you hear yourself? Do you even realize when you're being insulting? I mean, is it just instinct or is it deliberate?"

"Insulting? I walk into a room in my new hotel and find you practically salivating over some guy with a tool belt and a set of dimples, and I'm insulting?"

"You are, and what's worse is you don't see it," Jenny said and slapped both hands against his hard chest to shove her way free. He let her go. Taking a few steps away from him just because she *really* needed the distance right now, she faced him and said, "I'm here to do my job, Mike. You're my boss, not my lover."

"I remember it differently."

She flushed. *Damn it.* Jenny could actually feel heat race into her cheeks and could only hope that with the sunlight behind her, her face was in shadow enough that he wouldn't notice. "A couple of nights together doesn't make you my lover. It makes you…"

"Yeah?"

"A mistake," she finished. "Isn't that what you your-self called that first night? Oh, *and* the last one we spent together?"

He shoved both hands into his pockets and stared at her with an intensity she could feel. "I did. It was. That doesn't mean I enjoy standing by, watching you work some other poor guy into a frenzy."

"I had no idea I had so much power," Jenny said, shaking her head in disbelief. "Didn't realize I was so oblivious, either. I didn't see Rick—"

"Hmm. First-name basis already, huh?"

She ignored that and punched home what she most wanted to say. "I didn't see Rick in a frenzy—but you surely were."

"I was angry, not in a frenzy."

Was he jealous? Was it possible that Mike Ryan had seen her talking to Rick and had felt territorial over her? If he had, what did that mean? "Really. Angry that I was 'flirting' with someone other than you?"

"That you were flirting on the job, that's all," he said, and pulled both hands from his pockets to fold his arms across his chest. "Don't read more into this than there is."

"I don't think I am," Jenny said, moving close to him again. This was the weirdest conversation she'd ever had. Just a week or so ago, she'd pledged that she wouldn't be sleeping with Mike again. She already knew that this was a ticket to disaster. That the man had believed her to be a thief. Maybe he still did, she couldn't be sure. And yet, here she was, surrendering to the very need and hunger that had led her to his bed in the first place.

No. She couldn't. Not again. She would not allow herself to willingly walk right into more pain. With that thought firmly in place, she stopped where she was, looked up at Mike and said, "We're not going to do this again. I won't go to bed with you again."

"I didn't ask you to."

Now she smiled sadly. "Yeah, you did. In everything but words."

"Now you're a mind reader?"

"I don't have to be," Jenny told him and took a breath, hoping to ease the gnawing inside her. "I just know what happens when the two of us are alone together."

Seconds ticked past and the silence was heavy with a kind of tension that nearly vibrated in the air. Jenny held on to the ragged edges of the control that was rapidly slipping out of her grasp. If he pushed back, if he kissed her, then she'd be lost and she knew it.

"Damn it," he finally said in a gruff whisper. "You're not wrong." His gaze dropped from her eyes to her lips and back again. "I saw you with the carpenter and... Never mind. Like you said, none of my business."

Jenny nodded and said, "Let's just forget today, okay? We'll get the job finished tomorrow, then go home and things will get back to normal."

His blue eyes flashed with emotions that came and went so quickly, she couldn't identify them all, and maybe that was for the best.

"Normal." He nodded sharply. "Fine. We can finish

up at the new hotel by noon, probably. Then we'll head home and forget the whole damn trip."

Her heart gave a tug that unsettled her, but Jenny only forced a smile, keeping that small sliver of pain to herself. He wanted to forget the whole trip. Forget being with her, even that way-too-short moment they'd shared on the dock, where they'd talked like friends—or maybe more.

Forgetting wouldn't be easy, Jenny told herself, but it was the one sure path to sanity. Holding on to what she felt for Mike—feelings she didn't want to examine too closely—was only going to add to the misery later on. She had to find a way to let go of what-might-have-beens and focus instead on the cold, hard facts.

The man she wanted didn't want her beyond the nearest bed.

And that just wasn't good enough.

"So," Mike said, interrupting her thoughts, "I'll see you in the morning, then. Nine o'clock. Be ready to go to work."

"I will be." Once he was gone, Jenny dropped to the edge of the bed like a puppet whose strings had been cut.

This would be so much easier if only she didn't care.

Mike spent the evening working in his suite. He figured if he kept his mind busy with figures, budgets, plans for the future of their company, he'd have no time to think about Jenny. Or how she'd looked when he heard her describing the painting she wanted to do. He wouldn't hear the magic in her voice or see the interest in that carpenter's eyes when he watched her.

And he wouldn't keep seeing the look on her face when he had acted like some kind of demented comic-strip moron by accusing her of flirting with the guy. Hell, even if she had been, like she said, it was none of his damn business. But it sure as hell felt like it was. He'd hated watching that other man so focused, laser-like, on Jenny's face. Hated that he'd blamed *her* for whatever *he* was feeling.

"I don't know what's going on here," he muttered darkly, "but I don't like it." He'd always been in control. Of his feelings, his emotions—until Jenny. And what that meant, he didn't have a clue.

Mike scrubbed one hand across his face, pushed out of the desk chair and walked to the terrace. When his cell phone rang, he dragged it out of his pocket as he opened the sliding door and stepped into the teeth of a cold desert wind.

He glanced at the screen, then answered. "Hi, Mom."

"Hi. How's Vegas?"

"Laughlin."

"Same diff," she said and he could almost see her shrugging. "Sean told me you're out there inspecting the new hotel. What's it like?"

He dropped one hand on the iron railing, squinted into the wind and looked down to watch the river below froth beneath the hulls of flat-bottom boats taking tourists on a short ride. Neon fought against the stars for supremacy and won. On the Riverwalk, golden lamplight sifted onto the people strolling in and out of the shadows beside the river.

"It's run-down and sad right now, but I think it'll come together."

"Of course it will," his mother assured him. "My sons always do what they set out to do."

Mike smiled to himself.

"Sean says Jenny Marshall has some great ideas for

the artwork, too." She paused for a moment. "He says you and Jenny are there. Together."

"Does he?" Shaking his head, Mike ignored the blip of interest in Peggy Ryan's voice. He had to wonder if all mothers were as determined as his own to see her children married, with kids.

"Yes, he told me that you and Jenny would be working together for months on this new hotel…"

"Don't start," he warned her, amusement softening his words.

"Well, why shouldn't I?" she demanded with a huff. "You're not getting any younger, you know. And I've met Jenny. She's a nice girl. Talented. Pretty, too."

All true, he thought. She was also smart, opinionated, desirable and oh, yeah…untrustworthy. He scowled and remembered how cozy she'd looked with the damn carpenter today.

"Mom…"

"You can't fault a mother for hoping," she said, cutting him off before he could tell her to dial it back.

"Not interested in getting married, Mom," he said flatly. And she should know why, but he'd learned over the years that Peggy Ryan wanted nothing more than to forget the day that had changed everything for Mike.

There was a sigh in her voice when she said, "Fine. You are so hardheaded. Just like your father."

His frown deepened, but he didn't say anything. His mom didn't notice, or chose not to notice, because she rushed right on.

"I wanted to remind you, your dad's birthday is next week, and I want you and Sean both to show up, okay?"

Mike took a breath and blew it out. No way to avoid it and he knew it. But he never really looked forward to spending time with his father. It was…awkward. Uncomfortable.

Not that it had always been. Up until the year Mike turned thirteen, he'd thought of his father as his hero. Big, strong, with a wide smile and a kind nature, Jack Ryan was the kind of father most kids dream about. Jack had taught both of his sons to surf. A Little League coach, he'd spent hours at batting cages with them.

But the year he was thirteen, Mike had discovered that the father he idolized was also a liar. And that discovery had colored his image of his father ever since. He hadn't been able to forget or forgive. Jack had tried to close the distance between them many times, but Mike couldn't do it.

Memory was sometimes a hard thing and the images from the day when his father tumbled off that pedestal were as clear now as they had ever been.

"Oh, Mike," his mother said on a sigh, "I'm so sorry. You can't possibly know how sorry I am."

Mike stiffened. "You didn't do anything wrong, Mom."

"Yes," she argued. "I did. And I truly wish I could take it all back. Change that day."

"Yeah, well, we can't do that." Mike's hand tightened around his phone. "So let's just leave it in the past, okay?"

"I really wish you would, sweetie," Peggy said, then sighed again. "But fine. For now, I'll move on."

"It's appreciated."

"But I want you at your father's birthday dinner, Mike. No excuses. Sean's already promised to be here."

Of course he had. Sean didn't know what Mike did. He'd never told his younger brother about their father's fall from grace. Protecting Sean? Maybe. And maybe it was just that the thought of even more people knowing was too hard to take. Either way, though, Sean remained in the dark and that's how it would stay.

"Fine. I'll be there," he said, knowing his mother wouldn't stop until she'd gotten him to agree.

"Thanks, sweetie. We'll see you then." She paused. "Oh, and say hi to Jenny for me."

He hung up on her laughter. Shaking his head, he leaned his forearms on the terrace railing and watched the people below. Then he saw her. Jenny. Everything in him fisted as he watched her walk, alone, through the night, moonlight and neon playing in her hair.

Six

Normal was relative.

Jenny reminded herself several times during the following week that she and Mike were supposed to be back to "normal." And she supposed they were. For them.

The first day back, they stayed out of each other's way. But soon enough, work made that ploy impossible. While Jenny continued to work on the sketches of the Wise Woman for "The Wild Hunt" game, she was also going over her plans for the paintings at the new hotel. She'd taken so many pictures of the place, it was easy enough to figure out what she wanted where—it was simply time-consuming.

Then Mike got bogged down with calls from the contractor and plumber and electrician and the work on the game wasn't getting done, so Jenny volunteered to help. With her handling the Nevada hotel, it gave Mike time he needed to work with Sean and the marketing department on the cover design and the publicity campaign designed to push the game during release week.

Naturally, Jenny spent a lot of time in Mike's office fielding phone calls that she then had to tell him about, so they ended up spending hours together every workday. Yet what should have made them closer was instead highlighting the tension building between them.

Like now, Jenny thought as she sat down in front of Mike's desk. He was on the phone with one of the bloggers who posted about Celtic Knot, so Jenny had a minute to indulge herself in watching him.

His features were stony—his businessman face, she thought. Cool. No-nonsense. Unforgiving. His voice was clipped as he told the man what he wanted and expected, and Jenny had no doubt the blogger would do whatever Mike said. He had a knack for getting his way.

And for just a second, she wished *she* was his way.

Then he hung up and she forced her mind out of the lovely little daydreams it preferred and back to the business at hand.

"So, what've you got?" he asked, idly flipping a pen over and over between his fingers.

"Jacob says the painters can start next week," she said, checking her tablet and scrolling down to tick off information she had to give him. Jenny had spoken to the lead contractor so many times that week, she was beginning to think of the older man as family. "He also says the hotel employees you have living on-site have been helping the construction crew—lifting and toting mostly, but Jacob says they're really doing a lot to keep the work on schedule."

"Interesting," Mike admitted. "That wasn't part of our deal."

"Apparently, they got bored with just waiting for the new hotel to open." She shrugged and suggested, "They don't need to go out and find a new job, so maybe they're willing to help out, get the hotel open that much quicker. According to Jacob, they're doing a lot of the scut work, freeing up the crew to do the rehab."

Nodding, Mike said, "Make a note of the names of the guys who are doing the helping. We'll make sure they're paid for the extra work."

"Already done," she said.

He smiled and tossed the pen to the desk. "I like self-starters, people who are willing to step in and do what needs doing without being asked. Keep their names handy. We'll look at promotions when the hotel's up and running."

"I've got the list for you and the departments they worked in at the old hotel. I figured you'd want to do something like that."

"Impressive," he said with a nod of approval. "Are you sure you're an artist, not an admin?"

Surprised at the compliment, Jenny laughed. "Oh, artist, for sure. I don't mind helping you with this stuff, but if I had to keep track of everyone in the free world every day, it would drive me crazy."

"It does," Mike admitted. "I've been riding herd all week on bloggers, beta testers, the marketing guys and the design team working on the game cover. Sean hates the cover, I'm okay with it, but since neither of us is *happy* with it, they've got to go back to square one."

"What're they putting on the cover?"

"The forest, hints of a warrior stepping out from the trees, full moon…"

"Sounds a lot like the cover for 'Forest Run.'"

"Yes! That's exactly what I said." He shook his head, jumped up from his chair and paced to the window overlooking the yard and the blue, cloud-studded sky. "We need it different enough that people won't think they've already got it and similar enough that they know they'll be getting the same kind of fantasy they've become accustomed to."

"Hmm…" Jenny's gaze tracked him as he shifted impatiently from foot to foot at the tall window. If her gaze also dropped briefly to enjoy the view of his very nice behind, who could blame her? "What if we did something with the Wise Woman and the warrior together on the cover?"

He looked at her over his shoulder. "Go on."

"Maybe lightning flashing in the sky." Jenny closed her eyes briefly and could almost see it. "Magic shooting from her fingertips, wind lifting her hair, light gleaming off the warrior's sword…"

"I like it," he said, voice softer that it had been.

Jenny opened her eyes and looked into his and for a second or two convinced herself that she saw something…special. Then the moment was gone again because really, she shouldn't torture herself like that anyway.

"I'll give your ideas to the design team."

"Thanks," she said, pleasure making a warm knot in her chest.

"Hey, it's nice to talk to someone who doesn't need constant monitoring. Sometimes all I want to do is skeet shoot my cell phone."

"Understood. Completely." Didn't need to be monitored? Did that mean he was actually starting to trust her? *No,* she told herself, *don't get crazy.*

Going back to her tablet, Jenny continued. "We might as well finish this up. The engineers are on-site, working on the mechanisms for the river ghosts and ghouls. They say it'll take a couple months to get everything to be perfect, but again, according to Jacob, the engineers are excited."

"Okay, what else?"

"After all the positive stuff, there's a downside."

"Naturally," Mike said on a sigh. Easing one hip down onto the corner of his desk, he waved a hand. "Let's hear it."

"Jacob—wow, I've talked to him a lot this week—says there's a problem with the pipes."

"Great. What kind of problem?"

"The kind that means laying down new pipe. Mainly, the problem is the kitchen and the pool area. He says they'll probably last another five years, but after that, you'll need to redo the whole thing."

He laughed shortly, a scrape of sound with no trace of humor behind it. "Brady redid an entire fifteenth-century castle and those pipes were fine. I'm in charge of a hotel built in the 1950s and it's crap. What's up with that?"

Jenny shrugged. "Apparently castle pipes are made to last?"

"Apparently. Okay, what else does Jacob say?"

She winced a little. "He says to remind you that if you wait to do it, you'll have to pull out all the new tiles in the pool surround and take out a wall in the kitchen to get to everything. He suggests you do it all now."

"Of course he does," Mike said on a laugh. Then he

sighed and rubbed the back of his neck. "How the hell did we not find out about this problem during the inspection?" he muttered.

"Jacob says it's impossible to find stuff like this until you start getting beneath the surface." Jenny took a breath. This was going pretty well. They were in the same room and not sniping at each other. All she had to do was keep the focus on work and they'd be okay.

Of course, looking at him, it was hard to keep *thinking* about work. What she wanted to do was reach up and smooth his hair off his forehead. Step closer and feel his arms come around her. Lay her head on his chest and listen to his heartbeat.

And oh, dear God, she was sliding into a pool of something warm and tempting and way too dangerous. With that thought firmly in mind, she lifted her chin and stuck to business. "He says they didn't find the problems until they ripped out the kitchen floor to lay down a new subfloor before the tiles."

Mike nodded thoughtfully but didn't speak so she kept going.

"It's like all those rehab shows on HGTV. Couples buy this great house and they're redoing it and they find hideous things under the floor and behind the walls." She shuddered. "Makes you want to build new and avoid any old houses like the plague."

One dark eyebrow lifted and his mouth quirked. "Your apartment is an old one," he reminded her.

"Don't think I don't worry about that every time I see the people on TV finding mice and who knows what behind the walls." She shook her head hard and shivered again. "I try not to think about it."

"Don't blame you." Briefly, his eyes were warm,

nearly friendly. Then it was as if a shutter dropped down and suddenly, those blue eyes were cool and dispassionate again.

Jenny smothered a sigh.

"Jacob's right," Mike said finally. "We do the work now, make sure it's right. I want this hotel to be top-of-the-line all the way. No holding back. I'll call him, take care of it."

"Okay, good."

"Anything else?" He reached behind him for a bottle of water. Uncapping it, he took a long drink.

Jenny swallowed, too. Ridiculous that watching a man taking a drink could make her palms sweaty. Clearing her throat, she checked the tablet again. "Oh. Yeah. I talked to the interior designer you hired to furnish the hotel. She's not sure if you want contemporary furniture or something more—and I quote here—'antiquey' for the bedrooms."

"Antiquey?"

She shrugged. "Her word. I told her I thought you'd want something that feels old, almost otherworldly if she can manage it, but that I'd talk to you to make sure."

"You're right," he said and pushed off the desk. "I'll talk to her, but yeah, that's just what I want. Nothing fancy or fussy, but solid, heavy pieces that could be from the past or from the fantasy world we're re-creating."

"I think that's perfect."

Again, his mouth curved slightly and Jenny's heart did a slow tumble in her chest. It was ridiculous just how susceptible she was to this man.

"Good to know you agree," he said. "Because I need you to go with me to look at some furnishings. The designer's going to do most of it. She'll text me pictures of what she finds for approval, but Brady told me about a few places near here that had some great stuff he actually bought and had shipped to Ireland for the castle."

"He had stuff shipped? All the way to Ireland?"

"Well," he said, smiling a little, "not really. He had the movers stack it on the company jet and we flew it over ourselves. Still, would've been easier to buy it all there, but he found some nice stuff. Told me to check it out."

"Okay, when do you want to do that?"

"Next week's fine. We've still got plenty to arrange before then and…" he paused. "Aren't your new drawings of the Wise Woman due in tomorrow?"

"Yeah, they're nearly ready," she said, feeling a slight twinge of guilt. Usually, she turned her work in early, but she'd been so busy with everything else…

"If you need an extra day or two, don't worry about it." He walked closer. "I know you've been busy, picking up the slack on the hotel work."

"I don't mind helping."

He looked down at her. "And I appreciate it."

Her mouth was dry; her heart was pounding. She stared into his blue eyes and felt heat slide through her in a thick rush. Just being close to Mike was enough to weaken her knees—and her resolve. This was so not a good idea.

A quick knock sounded on the door and Sean walked in, already talking. "Hey, Mike? You're not going to believe what—" He stopped, looked from one to the other of them and asked, "Am I interrupting something?"

Mike took a single long step back, shook his head and said, "No. We were finished. Weren't we?"

Jenny shifted her gaze from Sean back to Mike and saw in his eyes that whatever had been looming between them was gone now. Probably a good thing, she acknowledged silently, but oh, she really wished Sean hadn't shown up.

"Yes," she said, when she found her voice, "we're finished."

And as she left the brothers alone, she thought those words had an eerie finality to them.

"Interesting," Sean mused as soon as Jenny had slipped off down the hall. He turned to look at his brother. "Something you want to share with the class?"

"No," Mike said shortly, hoping that Sean would let it go. But of course he didn't.

"I knew there was something going on between you two."

"You don't know anything about it," Mike insisted and walked around his desk to sit down.

"Oh, please. Am I blind?" Sean laughed and dropped into the chair opposite his brother. "That was an almost-kiss moment."

"Butt out, Sean."

Ignoring his brother, Sean continued. "Things were tense as hell between you guys before you went to Laughlin. When you came back it was tenser." He paused. "More tense? Whichever. You know what I mean."

"Yeah, I do, and I wish to hell you'd get what I mean when I tell you to back off."

"Oh, I get it," Sean assured him. "I'm just not listening. So tell me. What's with you and the oh-so-delicious Jenny Marshall?"

Mike's gaze snapped to his brother's. "Watch it."

"Oooh," Sean mused, grinning now. "Territorial. A good sign."

Well, walked right into that, didn't you? Mike's brain whispered.

"Damn it, Sean, stop." Mike tapped a few keys on his laptop, hoping to look too busy to sit and talk to his brother. "What did you come in here for in the first place?"

Still grinning, his brother eased off. "I wanted to tell you about the Wyoming property."

Mike frowned. "A problem?"

"Not with the place itself," Sean told him. "The sale went through, it's all ours. My problem is with the contractor."

"I'm having some issues there myself," Mike said, thinking about all the problems involved in getting a hotel up and running.

"Yeah, but your contractor's a guy. You can talk to a guy."

"Who's yours?"

"Supposedly the best one in the area. A woman. Kate Wells." Sean shook his head, jumped from the chair and paced the short distance to the window. "It's the middle of the damn winter and she wants to get started on the inside of the hotel. Says why waste time? Says she can't have the crew out working in the snow, but her schedule's clear now, so she wants to take her guys inside and start the renovation early."

"That's a problem?" Mike leaned back in his chair and tried to keep his mind on Sean's issues. Not easy when Sean was right about the almost-kiss moment. Seconds ago, he'd been about to—what? Kiss Jenny? Grab her, hold her? Close the office door and lay her down across his desk?

Damn it. Now he was hard and hot and it was even more difficult to focus on Sean.

"Sounds like a good plan to me," Mike said. "I like that this Wells woman has a good work ethic. Eager to get started, get a jump on things. Hell, she could have half of it done by the time the snow melts."

"Yeah?" Sean turned to look at him, exasperation clear on his face. "To get her started, I have to go the hell out there and work with her on the plans. Go through the hotel, see what's what, just like you did in Laughlin."

"Ah." In spite of everything else that was crowding his mind, Mike had to smile. "That's what this is about. You don't want to go to Wyoming."

"Of course I don't," Sean snapped. "There's *snow* there. Lots of it. Have you looked outside *here* today?" He waved one hand at the window behind him. "Blue skies, puffy white clouds, *sun*. It's almost eighty today. You know what it is in Wyoming? I do. I checked. It's twenty-eight. That's the *high*."

Mike chuckled and at his brother's glare, tried his best to muffle it and failed. "It's not forever, Sean. You go out, do the work, come back. At the most, you'll miss a few days of surfing. You'll survive."

"Thanks for the support," his brother muttered. "I'd have to take one of the artists to look the place over for murals, too. Hey." His face brightened. "Think Jenny'd be interested in a quick trip to snow country? Her sketches are great, she'd probably be a big help—"

"No." Mike cut him off before he could get going. Damned if he was going to sit back and have Jenny fly off to Wyoming with Sean. They'd be alone on the plane, at the hotel… No.

"Well, that was decisive."

"Just get one of the others to go with you."

"Not going to be easy to coax someone off a beach and into a snowbank."

"We've all got our problems," Mike told him, and instantly, his mind shot back to Jenny.

The problem there was he couldn't stop thinking about her, wanting her, needing her. And he knew damn well that there was no place in his life for her. He already knew that she was a liar. Okay, fine, she hadn't lied *lately*. But that didn't mean a damn thing. All it told him was that more lies were coming. When? What kind? And how the hell could he be so damn interested in a woman he *knew* he couldn't trust?

Sean came back, sat in the chair again, braced his forearms on the desk and leaned in. "Talk to me, Mike. What is going on with you? What's the deal with Jenny?"

Tempting to confide in Sean, but at the core of it, Mike wasn't a big sharer. He kept his thoughts, his emotions, locked down tight. Not many people got past the wall he'd built around himself. He loved his brother, but there were some things a man just didn't discuss. With anyone.

Shaking his head, Mike scraped one hand across his face. "Nothing I want to talk about, okay?"

Sean watched him for a long minute before saying, "All right. But I'm here when you want to talk. Remember that."

"I will."

"Okay," Sean said. "You're going to Mom and Dad's tonight, right? Not backing out?"

From one problem to another. Mike had considered blowing off his father's birthday dinner. He didn't need the aggravation piled on top of everything else going on. All he needed was to stoke the fire burning at the back of his brain. But if he didn't show up, his mother would make him pay. Somehow. Didn't seem to matter how old you were, your mother retained power over you. And Peggy Ryan had no difficulty wielding that power.

"Yeah, I'm going."

"Wow, feel the enthusiasm."

Mike glared at him. "I'm going. Should be good enough."

"You keep saying things that make me want more information," Sean told him, leaning back in his chair. He kicked his feet up and crossed them on the corner of Mike's desk. "You don't want to talk about Jenny. How about you tell me why you're always pissed at Dad."

"Not going there, either."

"You are not an easy person to have for a brother," Sean told him with a shake of his head. "You've got more secrets than the CIA."

"And the nature of a secret is, it's not talked about."

"That's what you think," Sean countered. "You know I could find out. I could just go to Mom."

"Don't." He didn't want his mother reminded of old pain. Didn't want her to have to tell her other son the things she'd inadvertently told Mike so many years before.

"Just 'don't'? That's all I get? What the hell, Mike? You've been at war with Dad for years and you won't say why." Sean braced both hands on the edge of the desk. "If you know something I should, then tell me."

Mike studied his brother for a long minute. During that short period of time, his brain raced through the familiar scenarios he knew he would be facing over dinner. Strained conversations, his mother trying to be overly bright and happy, his father sending Mike covert glances.

It wouldn't be pleasant. Wouldn't be easy. But he would play the game for his mother's sake.

As far as his little brother went, though, there was just no reason for Sean to have to battle the same emotions that Mike did when the family was together. "Sean, believe me, you don't want to know. So just let it go, all right?"

For a second or two, Sean looked as though he'd argue, but finally, he nodded and stood up. "Fine. But try to remember. I might be your younger brother...but I'm not a kid you need to protect."

Maybe not, Mike thought, but there was no reason to shatter his illusions, either.

A few hours later, Jenny jolted out of the movie she was watching when someone knocked at her door. Wearing her flannel sleep pants and a white tank, she was curled up on the couch with a bowl of popcorn and a glass of wine. Not working. Trying not to think. Just immersing herself in a few harmless explosions on the television.

She wasn't expecting anyone, so naturally, her very excellent imagination conjured up images of roving pirates, rabid serial killers or maybe even an escapee from a mental institution, all crowded together on her tiny front porch.

She wasn't the nervous Nellie type, but when she was alone at night, she often thought about getting a dog. A big one. But for now, she got up, looked out the curtains and sighed, both relieved and annoyed.

Mike.

At least he wasn't a marauder, but why did he have to show up when she looked hideous? No makeup, her hair a messy tumble of curls and wearing her *Star Wars* flannels? And what did it matter? she asked herself. He'd made it clear he wasn't interested, so let him see the real her…flannel jammies and all.

She opened the door and looked up at him.

"You don't ask who it is before you open a door?" he demanded, blue eyes flashing.

"Wow. Hello to you, too."

"Come on, Jenny. You're a woman living alone. Be smart."

"I looked out the window and saw you."

"Oh, that's all right, then."

"Thanks very much." One hand on the open door, one on the jamb, she asked, "What are you doing here, Mike?"

"Honestly," he said, "I don't know. Just had dinner with the family at my folks' house and didn't want to go home yet. I drove around for a while and ended up here."

Fascinating.

He wore a black jacket over a white shirt, open at the collar, with black jeans and boots that looked as if they'd seen a lot of miles. His hair had been ruffled by the wind and his eyes looked…empty. His features were tight, his shoulders tense, and Jenny thought he was on the verge of leaving. She didn't want him to.

"Do you want a glass of wine?" she asked.

His gaze fixed on hers. "That'd be good. Thanks."

Polite, but distant. That, plus a little outright suspicion, she was used to. Tonight, though, there was a sadness about him that she'd never seen before and Jenny felt a flicker of worry she knew he wouldn't appreciate.

He stepped inside, and she closed and locked the door behind him.

"You were at your parents' house, you said. Are they okay? Sean?"

He looked at her. "Yeah. They're all fine."

She tipped her head to one side and studied him. "You're not."

He laughed shortly and scraped one hand along his jaw. "I don't like being read that easily, but no, I guess not."

It was the first time she could ever remember seeing Mike Ryan vulnerable in any way. Normally he was so in charge, so much the stalwart head of a billion-dollar company, that seeing his features strained and closed off was unsettling. She'd rather have him raging at her than see him looking so lost.

"I shouldn't have come here—" he said abruptly.

But he had, Jenny told herself. For whatever reason, he'd been upset and he'd come to *her*. That had to mean something, didn't it? "Stay. Take off your jacket. Sit down. Have a glass of wine, Mike."

It took a moment or two, but he finally nodded and said, "Okay, thanks."

He shrugged out of his jacket and draped it across the back of a chair, then looked around the room as if seeing it for the first time. It wasn't his first visit, though. He'd been here before. The night they'd— Whoops. Probably not a good idea to think about that right now.

Mike stood in the middle of the small living room, glanced at the popcorn and her wineglass and then shifted his gaze to hers. "Movie night?"

She shrugged. "I just wanted to relax, you know. A lot going on right now…"

"Tell me about it." He sat on the couch, took a handful of popcorn and watched the movie playing out on the screen.

She went to the kitchen to get him that wine, then walked back to the living room and handed him a glass of chardonnay. He took a sip, gestured with the glass toward the TV and asked, *"Die Hard?"*

She smiled and sat on the other end of the couch. "It's my feel-good movie. You know, Christmas, good guys beating the bad guys…"

"And lots of stuff blowing up."

"Exactly." She grinned and sipped her wine.

"I didn't know you liked action movies."

"There's a lot you don't know about me."

"And some I do," he said, a frown flattening his mouth.

"Or think you do," she countered. She wasn't a liar and a thief, and she felt that somewhere inside him, he knew that or he wouldn't have been sitting on her couch.

"Touché." He nodded, glanced at the television again. "One guy going against a whole crew."

"To save his wife," she said with a satisfied sigh. "It's romantic."

He chuckled. "Romance and bombs?"

"Works for me."

His gaze shifted to the flannel pants she wore. "Darth Vader pajamas?"

She grinned. "They're cozy." And were a gift from her uncle Hank, but she doubted he'd want to hear that.

"I don't know what to think about you, Jenny," he said.

"Good. I'm glad. That means you're not entirely sure you should think what you used to think because now you think your thinking might have been wrong."

He blinked at her, then shook his head. "I actually followed that."

Turning his head again, he stared at the television. In the flickering light, darkness passed over his features, highlighting the shadows crouched in his eyes.

"Why are you really here, Mike?"

Slowly, he looked back at her. "You know why."

There was that wild flutter and rush of anticipation moving through her stomach again. She took a swallow of wine to ease her suddenly dust-dry throat, then set the glass on the table in front of her.

Jenny knew exactly what he was talking about. She'd felt it in the office today. Before Sean came in, there had been a slow, simmering burn between Mike and her, and that fire was still there, hot as ever. Acting on it would be a huge mistake. But *not* acting on it was driving her crazy.

"Yes," she said softly, holding his gaze with her own. "I know."

"So the question is," Mike asked, voice low and deep and intimate, "do you want me to leave?"

"No."

"Thank God." He set his glass down and reached for her.

Pushing the popcorn out of the way, Jenny went into his arms; all the while her mind called out a warning she refused to heed. She didn't want to be wise. Didn't want to be smart. She wanted Mike and that just wouldn't change.

But it was more than that, she admitted silently as Mike's mouth claimed hers. She leaned into him, opened to him, and felt the heat within build into something that was both wilder and more…steady than anything she'd ever known before.

Her breath caught, as understanding dawned. Her mind spun and she clung to Mike because he was the only steady point in her universe.

She loved Mike Ryan.

Her brain went into overdrive in the span of a single heartbeat. The months of working at Celtic Knot, watching Mike work with young artists, encouraging them. Seeing his dedication to his work, his brother and friend. Knowing that he didn't trust her, but having him give her the opportunity to work on his hotel in spite of it all.

He didn't trust her.

Didn't love her.

There was misery lying in wait, and Jenny knew it. But her whole life had been spent wanting the very feelings that were crashing down around her right now.

So she'd risk the pain to have this one moment—even if Mike never knew what was shining in her heart.

Seven

A few days later, Mike was at his desk when the video chat bell on his phone went off. He hit Answer and his brother's face appeared on the screen.

"I hate Wyoming."

Mike laughed. Sean looked haggard, on edge. His eyes were narrowed, whisker stubble covered his jaws and the scowl he wore looked as if it had been permanently etched into his face.

"Don't hold back, tell me how you really feel."

"Funny." Sean glanced over his shoulder, then back into the camera. "It hasn't stopped snowing since I got here. There's like three feet of snow piling up out there and it's still coming down. I don't think it'll ever stop."

"Sounds cold."

"Hah! Beyond cold. Beyond freezing. I'm wearing two sweaters *inside*."

Chuckling, Mike asked, "What's it like when you're not bitching about how cold you are?"

Sean sighed then grudgingly admitted, "It's pretty. Lots of trees. Lots of open land. And who knew the sky was so big when you get out of the city?"

Mike smiled. He'd discovered that for himself when he and Jenny were in Laughlin. Of course, allowing Jenny into his mind meant opening himself up to the memories that never really left him. Her smile. Her eyes. The feel of her skin against his. The soft sigh of her breath as she surrendered to him. Stopping in at her house after work, spending the evening watching movies, making love, talking about the work, the hotel. Talking about everything except for the fact that he couldn't trust her.

Pushing those thoughts away, he asked, "What's the hotel itself like, Sean?"

"Big. Cold. Empty." Sean blew out a frustrated breath and pushed one hand through his hair. "But the bones are good. A lot of work to do to turn it into a 'Forest Run' fantasy."

"And is Kate Wells up to the task?"

"To hear her tell it," Sean muttered. "Anyway, there's a hundred and fifty guest rooms and they all need work."

"If we go with your idea to hold our own game con on the property, we'll need more rooms. Are there other hotels close by?"

"No. We're ten miles from the closest town and it's got two B and Bs and one motel right off the highway."

It was Mike's turn to frown. "Sean, we can't go with a big conference if there's nowhere for people to stay." He took a breath and spoke again before Sean could suggest camping. "And don't say people can pitch tents."

Sean laughed. "Just because I like camping doesn't

mean I want strangers staying all over the property. Anyway, there's a bigger city about twenty-five miles from here, with more hotels and Kate—the contractor—had another idea on that, too."

"What's she thinking?" Mike picked up his coffee and took a long drink.

Sean's frown deepened. "Is that a cappuccino? You bastard."

"I'll enjoy it for you."

"Thanks." Shaking his head, Sean said, "Kate thinks we should put in some small cabins, behind the main lodge, staggered back into the forest. Give people more privacy, a sense of being out in the open..."

Mike nodded, thinking about it. "It's a good idea."

"Yeah, I know."

"Yet you don't look happy about it."

"Because she was so damn sure she was right," Sean told him. "It's hard agreeing she was."

"Sounds like you're having a great time," Mike said with another deliberate sip of his hot coffee.

Sean's eyes narrowed into slits. "This woman is the most hardheaded person I've ever dealt with and that includes *you*."

"As long as she does good work, that's all you should care about."

"Yeah, yeah. She wants to get her crew in here next week and start in on the rehab and I don't see a problem with it." He paused and ran one finger around the collar of his black sweater. "As long as I can oversee it from California."

"Okay, but since you didn't take any of the artists with you, what'll she do about the painting we'll need done?"

"Come on," Sean said. "I couldn't bring an artist out

here when everyone's doing the final run on 'The Wild Hunt.'"

True. It was bad timing all the way around, really. Sean had had to get to the next hotel and every artist in the company was focused on the finishing touches of the game that would be released next.

"Anyway," Sean continued, "how hard is it to leave walls blank? They can paint it white or something and then when we bring the artists in, they can change it to whatever."

"That'll work. You still coming home tomorrow?"

"That's the plan, thank God," Sean said. "Kate's outside, bringing her truck around. Naturally, it's still snowing."

"If it makes you feel any better, it's seventy-five here today."

"Great. Thanks. That just caps it." A door slammed somewhere. Sean looked to one side and shouted, "What?"

"What is it?" Mike asked.

"Karma probably," Sean told him, his expression disgusted. "Kate just heard on the truck radio that the pass down the mountain is closed. I'm snowed in."

Mike tried not to, but his brother looked so furious and frustrated, he couldn't hold back the laughter. Even as Sean gave him a dirty look, Mike held up one hand and tried to stop laughing. "Sorry, sorry."

"How is this funny?" Sean demanded. "I'm trapped in an empty hotel with a crabby contractor and a mountain of snow outside the door."

"Clearly," Mike said finally, "it's only funny from California. But have you got food, heat?"

"Yeah," Sean said, then spoke to someone in the room with him. "Come here for a minute. Meet my brother."

A second or two later, a woman popped onto the screen. Pretty, with a heart-shaped face and a wide mouth, she had black hair and eyes as blue as Sean's. She was wearing a baseball cap pulled low on her forehead and what looked like a heavy green sweater.

"Hi, I'm Kate and you're Mike," she said, words tumbling over each other. "Nice to meet you, but we don't have a lot of time to talk. There's firewood outside, we need to bring it in before the rest of the storm hits. Don't worry, though. There's plenty of food since I make sure my crew is fed while they work and we've been out here this last week taking measurements and getting ideas about the work."

"Okay." Mike threw that word in fast, thinking he probably wouldn't have another chance to speak. He was right.

"The storm'll blow through in a day or two and the plows will have the pass cleared out pretty quickly, so you can have your brother back by the end of the week."

"Okay..."

Sean grabbed the phone and told Kate, "I'll be right there to help. Yeah. Okay." When he looked back at Mike, he was shaking his head. "I was this close—" he held up two fingers just a breath apart "—from getting outta Dodge. Now I don't know when I'll get out. Tell Mom not to worry and don't bother calling me. I'm going to shut off the cell phone, conserve power."

"Okay." In spite of the fact that he'd been amused only a few minutes ago by Sean's situation, now Mike wondered. "You sure you'll be all right?"

Sean laughed now. "I'm the outdoors guy, remember? There may not be any waves to surf out here, but I'll be fine. I've been camping in worse situations than I've got here. At least we have a roof and plenty of beds to choose from. I'll call when I can. Just keep a cappuccino hot for me because I'll be back as soon as I can."

"I will. And, Sean?" Mike added, "Don't kill the contractor."

Smirking, Sean said, "I make no promises."

Two weeks later, Jenny was fighting a resilient flu that just refused to go away.

Every morning her stomach did an oily slide toward rebellion and every morning she fought it back. She was simply too busy to let some determined bug knock her flat. So she went to work, forced herself to eat and by evening was usually feeling if not great, at least better. Until the next day when it would all start again.

Hunched over her tablet, Jenny made notes on the hotel murals, then shifted files and added a few more finishing touches on the Wise Woman sketches for "The Wild Hunt." The witch was great and the addition to the script had really given the game that extra punch.

She'd even played the beta game the day before herself just to see how difficult it really was to find the extra runes that would free the witch. It was a challenge. So she knew the hardcore gamers among their fans were going to love it.

Yawning, she shut down that program and called up the list of artists and painters she'd developed. She'd need to hire at least three or four people to help her with the murals and would have to check out their qualifications first.

Sunlight slanted in through the windows of the graphic arts department and all around her conversations and ripples of laughter rang out. Fingers hit keyboards, rock music played softly from one of the cubicles, and here and there in the room people bent their heads together to go over the work.

None of the distractions bothered her because Jenny was used to working with background noise. She'd never yet met an artist who did their best work in sterile silence. So while her friends and colleagues worked the games, Jenny went to artists' websites.

She looked at portfolios, studied techniques, then checked the artists' bios and read about their backgrounds. Artists were usually solitary people, but she needed those who could work with others and take instruction. That was the hard part and she knew it. Most artists treasured their own vision of whatever they were working on at the time and didn't much care for someone else coming in and telling them what to do next.

But in this case, whoever was hired had to be willing to go along with the plans for the murals and portraits. They had to stick to the creative brief that Jenny was still finishing and not waste time arguing over the direction of the project.

She yawned and scrolled through the bio of a Nevada artist who specialized in fantasy paintings. His work was stellar but the smugness of his bio convinced Jenny he wasn't a team player.

"Next," she muttered and closed the page before moving on to another name on her list. She only needed to find one more artist and then she could get moving on the actual painting on-site.

"Hey, Jen—"

She looked up and smiled at Casey Williams. New to the company, Casey was a talented intern. She'd only worked at Celtic Knot for a couple of months, but she'd slid right into the mix as if she'd always been there. About twenty-five, Casey was married with a baby son. She had long dark hair that lay in a single braid across her shoulder. Her T-shirt was bright red, her jeans were a faded gray and her flip-flops revealed the green polish on her toes.

"What's up, Casey?" Jenny smothered another yawn behind her hand.

"Dave wants to know if you've finished tweaking the Wise Woman—"

"Yes, just a few minutes ago. I'll email the file to him."

"Cool. And I just want to say, I love your vision of her." Casey's hands were gripped together at her waist. "I saw the prelim sketches and they're amazing. It was a great idea to include her as a surprise for gamers. But the images are what really grabbed me. She's powerful and beautiful and— You don't look so hot."

Jenny laughed shortly. And here she thought she'd been so good about covering up how miserable she felt. "Thanks."

"No." Casey backtracked fast. "No, I mean, you look like you still don't feel well."

"Actually, I really don't," Jenny said, shaking her head, then regretting the abrupt motion because it wobbled her already unsteady stomach a little. For days, she'd been dragging around the office, trying to concentrate on the work even while her body continually reminded her she should be home in bed.

"Um…" Casey glanced around her, as if checking to make sure no one could overhear them. Then she sat down on the edge of a chair and leaned in closer. "I know we don't know each other very well yet, so this is probably out of line. But you've been feeling sick for a week or more now, right?"

"Yes…" Jenny said, wondering where this was going.

"I know this is none of my business." Casey took a breath and then let it go. "But I know the signs because I lived them myself a year ago."

Confused, Jenny asked, "What're you talking about? What signs?"

"Is it possible," Casey asked gently, "that this isn't the flu? That maybe you're pregnant?"

Shock held Jenny in place for a slow count of ten. Her mind, however, was racing. Thinking. *Counting.*

"Oh, my God." Panic rose up and choked off the nausea in the pit of her stomach. She did some fast calculating again, running through the numbers, the weeks, the possibilities. And ended up wheezing for air.

"Yeah," Casey whispered, nodding in understanding, "that's what I thought."

Oh, God, how far out of it was she that another woman was the one who had to tell her she was pregnant? How had she missed this? But even as she asked herself that, she knew the answer. She hadn't figured it out because she hadn't wanted to. Her relationship with Mike was so…tricky, a pregnancy was going to change everything.

Casey was still talking; excited, comforting, worried, Jenny couldn't be sure. All she really heard was a buzz of sound from the other woman. It was as if Jenny's head were filled with cotton, muffling everything but the pounding of her own heart.

Pregnant? By her *boss*?

It was more than possible, she knew. Instantly, her mind dragged up images from over the past few weeks. Incredible sex, sharing moments with Mike that she wouldn't trade for anything. They'd used protection of course, but no contraception worked 100 percent guaranteed. Would Mike believe that, though? No, he wouldn't.

Oh, God.

She blinked and the office came back into focus. She looked at Casey, and saw the woman's encouraging smile. All around her, life went on as usual, with no one but Casey aware that Jenny's world had just taken a major shift. She took a breath, tried to calm down, but that wasn't going to happen. Not until she knew, for sure. She could suspect she was pregnant, but until she knew without a doubt, she wouldn't be able to think clearly. Wouldn't be able to face Mike, with this suspicion simmering in her bloodstream. She had to know. Now. Suddenly, she couldn't sit there a moment longer.

Jenny grabbed her purse out of her desk drawer, then lunged to her feet. "You know, I really think I should just go home early."

"Are you worried?" Casey asked gently. "About how your boyfriend's going to take the news? I was nervous before I told my husband." She smiled to herself. "There was no reason to be. He was excited. Happy."

Mike wouldn't be. But Jenny couldn't say that because no one in the office knew she and Mike were together. Oh, this just got more and more complex.

Still, she forced a smile she didn't feel and lied to the nice woman still watching her. "I'm sure you're right and he will be. But right now, I think I just need to lie down for a while."

"That's a good idea," Casey said and stood up, too. "Take care of yourself and if you need anything—" She shrugged. "Call me, okay?"

"Sure. I will. Um, thanks, Casey."

"No problem. Drive safe."

Drive, Jenny told herself as she left the office and headed for the parking lot. Straight to a drugstore where she'd buy a few pregnancy tests and take them all. For the first time in her life, she was actually hoping she had the flu.

She didn't.

An hour later, Jenny looked at the five test strips lined up on her bathroom counter. Every last one of them was positive. She hadn't trusted one kind of test, either. She'd bought different ones, tried them all. And they all proved her suspicions right.

"I guess that's it, then," she murmured, lifting her gaze to her own reflection in the bathroom mirror. "I'm going to have a baby. Mike's baby."

Both hands covered her flat belly as if cradling the child within. She waited, meeting her own eyes in the mirror, trying to decipher the myriad emotions racing through her. Sure, panic was in there, but it wasn't uppermost in her mind. First and most important, there was *excitement*.

This wouldn't be easy, she admitted silently, but nothing great ever was. There was a lot to think about, to plan for. First, of course, she had to tell Mike. She wouldn't even try to keep this from him, even knowing how he was going to react.

Her heart hurt as she thought about the confrontation that would come soon. He'd never trusted her and this news was going to convince him that he had been right about her all along. She still had to tell him that she was carrying his child. Even if he wanted nothing to do with her afterward. Even if he walked out and never looked back.

She took a breath to steady herself, but the twinges of pain still squeezed her heart. Mike wasn't going to be happy. But Jenny was. There had never been a future for her and the man she loved, but now when he walked away, she would have something of him, forever. A baby. Her own child. Her own family. Someone to love. Someone who would love her.

She hadn't planned this, but now that the baby was here, she wouldn't change it, either.

"I promise, I want you," she whispered, voice soft with wonder as her palms stroked her belly. "You'll be loved and you'll never have to worry about me walking away. About being left alone. You'll be safe, I swear it."

She lifted her chin, stiffened her spine and resolved then and there that no matter what Mike said, what he tried to make her feel, she wouldn't lose this excitement. This sense of pure joy that was already whipping through her like lightning strikes. She hadn't expected this pregnancy, but she would never regret it.

She would give this child the life she had always wanted. It would grow up loved and secure and it would never, ever doubt its mother's love.

Jenny took a steadying breath and tried to steer her celebratory thoughts back down into more immediate concerns. Like facing Mike—and the possibility that she would have to change jobs. Even if he didn't fire her and who knew, he very well might, working at Celtic Knot over the next few months could be very uncomfortable.

But before she made any decisions, she had to tell Mike.

Jenny watched her reflection wince. That conversation wasn't going to be pretty. He would never believe she hadn't planned this pregnancy. And any semblance of warmth that had sprung up between them over the past few weeks was going to dissipate.

She hated knowing that. Hated understanding that her time with Mike was going to end. But not only did she love the man, she *knew* him. So she had to prepare herself for the fact that once he knew the truth, all of her fantasies would be over.

When her cell phone rang she went out to answer it. Seeing Mike's name on the screen didn't even surprise her. Of course he would call when she was thinking about him. Of course she wouldn't have time to get used to this staggering news before having to tell him and weather the inevitable fallout. But maybe it was better this way. Worrying over the coming confrontation would only tie her up in knots anyway.

Steeling herself, she answered. "Hi, Mike."

"Jenny, are you all right?" She closed her eyes at the sound of his voice. At the concern ringing in his tone. "Casey says you went home sick."

Sick. Well, technically, her stomach was still feeling a little iffy, but it was so much more.

"I'm okay, but, Mike," she said, mentally preparing herself for what was to come, "we have to talk."

An hour later, Mike stood in her living room staring down at the five test sticks she'd laid out on the coffee table. Brain burning, heart pounding, Mike stared at the evidence in front of him and still couldn't quite bring himself to believe it. He took a few deep breaths, willing himself to calm down, to beat back the sense of betrayal and suspicion that slapped at him.

"Pregnant?" He shifted his gaze to the woman across

the room from him. Her blond hair curled around her head. Her blue eyes were wide and shone with an innocence he couldn't trust. She wore those silly flannel pants and a yellow tank top that bared her shoulders and hugged her generous breasts. His gaze dropped to her belly briefly as he tried to imagine a child—*his* child—nestled inside.

He couldn't do it.

"How the hell did that happen?"

Her eyebrows lifted. "Really?"

He pushed both hands through his hair and scrambled for patience. "I know *how*, so don't get cute. But we used a condom. Every time."

"I know," Jenny said, wrapping her arms around her middle almost defensively, "but nothing's a hundred percent."

"Well, they damn well should be," he argued. What the hell as the point of using a damn condom if they didn't do their job? "Unless…" Mind clicking along, racing down dark, twisted, tangled roads, he said, "You had those condoms in your drawer."

"So?"

He didn't answer that question. Instead, he turned and stalked into her bedroom, tore open the drawer and grabbed one of the condoms still there. Had they been damaged somehow? Had she found a way to sabotage them so… He saw the date stamped on the bottom of the foil.

"What're you doing?" Jenny asked as she came into the room behind him.

"I thought maybe you'd done something to these," he muttered, turning to look at her, still holding the damn condom. "I don't know, poked holes in them with a needle or something."

She gaped at him. "Are you serious?"

He ignored that, just as he paid no attention to the look of astonishment on her face. She wasn't an innocent and he should have remembered that before allowing himself to slide into an affair that could only end badly. "Turns out you didn't have to. How the hell long have you had these things?"

She blinked in confusion, then said, "What does that have to do with anything?"

"Just answer the question."

Frowning at him, she said, "They were party favors at a bachelorette party I went to five years ago."

"Five years." Nodding, he curled his fingers around the condom package and squeezed.

"Does that matter?"

A short, sharp laugh shot from his throat. "Yeah. It matters. Especially since they *expired* five years ago." He couldn't believe this.

"What do you mean?" She practically pried his fingers apart to snatch the packet from him. "Condoms can *expire*?"

"You thought they lasted forever?"

"No," she said, "I never thought about it. Why would I? It's not like they have to be refrigerated or anything. Who would expect they could go bad? They're in their own little foil packs for heaven's sake."

"That's just perfect," he muttered and thought back to the first night with her here, at her house, and how damned grateful he'd been that she had condoms on hand. He'd never checked them out. Never thought to make sure they were good.

He scrubbed both hands across his face and told himself this was what he got for going against his own instincts. He'd wanted her. Had to have her. Even knowing that she was a liar. Now he was paying the price for following his own needs.

"It's probably why your friend gave them away as party favors," he muttered darkly. "Because they were no good, she got 'em cheap.

"But why would you hold on to them?"

"I didn't think about it," she said with a shake of her head. "I just tossed them into the drawer and never gave it another thought."

"Perfect," he muttered, scraping one hand across his face.

"You knew they were no good," he said, voice deep, dark. Anger bubbled in his gut until it was a thick, hot brew that spilled through his veins. "You knew what would happen if we used them and you were good with that, weren't you?"

"Are you serious?"

"Damn right, I'm serious." He crowded in on her, forcing her to back up until her legs hit the mattress and she plopped down onto it. "This was all a setup, wasn't it? Right from the beginning."

"What *all* are you talking about?" she demanded, glaring up at him. "You mean, you coming to my house, willingly going to my bed? That *all*?"

"Us meeting in Phoenix. You coming to work at Celtic Knot. It's all been building to this, right? Why the hell else would you come to work for me after what happened when we met?"

"You are seriously paranoid," she snapped, tossing her hair out of her eyes so she could glare at him.

"Right. I'm paranoid, but you're pregnant, so maybe I'm not crazy, huh?" He leaned over her until their faces were just a breath apart. The smell of her invaded his senses and threw gasoline on the fire inside him. Even furious, even staggered by her news, Mike could admit to wanting her. To needing her. And that fried him.

"All you needed to do was get me in here, to use the damn useless condoms so you could get pregnant." He was so angry, the edges of his vision were blurred. His breath came fast and hard, his heartbeat thundered and desire tangled with fury until his whole body practically vibrated.

She shoved at him and he backed up just far enough for her to clamber off the bed and gain her feet again. "My God, do you really think you're that great a prize? Do you know how many times you've insulted me by calling me a thief? And that's supposed to endear you to me somehow?"

"Yet you slept with me anyway and here we are," he reminded her, in spite of the sparks flashing in her eyes.

"You're right," she said, sarcasm dripping from her words. "How clever I must be. And psychic as well to *know* that the great Mike Ryan would one day deign to visit my little apartment. Would allow me to seduce him with my trickery and feminine wiles. How brilliant of me to have faulty condoms so I could fool him into impregnating me. My God, I'm *amazing*."

It sounded ludicrous even to him, but Mike couldn't let it go completely. His mind worked, with two opposing voices shouting, demanding to be heard. But the calm, cool, rational part of him was buried beneath the facts he couldn't forget. She'd lied to him the first time he met her. She'd come to work at his company in spite of that.

She'd wormed her way onto his hotel design team. She'd made herself *important*. But he'd kept her on. Hadn't told Sean to fire her. Why? Because she had gotten into his blood whether he'd wanted her there or not.

Now she was pregnant.

He looked down at her and the flash in her blue eyes did nothing to ease the anger bubbling and frothing inside him. It didn't help to know that even as furious as he was, he could still look at her and need her.

"No matter what you think," she said tightly, "I didn't trick you. I didn't set up a *trap* to catch the mighty and elusive Mike Ryan."

"Well, since you're so honest," he ground out, "I'll just believe you, okay?"

"You should but you won't," she told him, shaking her head, sending those curls that drove him crazy into a wild dance about her head. She underlined each of her words with a determined tap of her index finger against his chest. "Do you really think I would trap a man who doesn't want me? I've got more self-respect than that, thanks."

Jenny stood there facing him, chin lifted, eyes narrowed and hot with banked fury. She looked beautiful and strong, and it took everything he had to fight the urge to grab her and pull her in close. Jenny Marshall got to him like no one else ever had and he hated admitting that, even to himself.

Shaking his head, he took a mental step backward and told her, "It's not going to work. You're not getting money out of me and I won't marry you."

Her head jerked back as if he'd slapped her, but she recovered fast, he had to give her that.

"I don't want *anything* from you. As for marrying me?

Who asked you to?" she demanded and whirled around. She left the bedroom, walked into the living room, and he followed because what the hell else was he going to do?

She stopped in front of the windows and with the last of the sun's rays silhouetting her in gold, she looked at him and said, "I wouldn't marry you on a bet, Mike. You think I'd actually trap a man who doesn't want me into a marriage that would be a misery? No, thanks. I don't need you to take care of me or my baby, Mike."

Now it was his turn to feel insulted. Whatever he did or didn't feel for Jenny, she was carrying *his* kid and she'd better get used to that from the jump. "You can't keep my child from me, Jenny, so don't even try."

"Who said I would?" Shaking her head, she said, "You keep putting words in my mouth. So why not just stop trying to think for both of us? Telling you about the baby was the right thing to do. If you want to see our child, that's your choice. But you don't call the shots here, Mike, and I think you should leave."

He didn't want to. But staying here angry wouldn't help the situation any. He needed some air. Needed to think. But when he walked out of her house and heard the door slam shut behind him, Mike acknowledged that the real problem was that he needed her, too.

Eight

"You're pregnant?"

Jenny sighed and waited for her uncle to finish ranting. Right after Mike left, she had driven south to her uncle's house on Balboa Island. She'd needed…support, and she'd known she'd find it here. At least, she would once her uncle was finished calling down curses on Mike Ryan's head.

Her gaze tracked the older man as he paced around his living room. Just as when she'd told Mike about the baby, she'd come expecting this exact reaction. The man had never forgiven Mike for accusing Jenny of trying to use him. And this situation wasn't making her uncle any fonder of Mike Ryan.

"He turned on you, didn't he?"

Jenny winced and her uncle saw it. His gaze narrowed and his features tightened into lines of fury.

"I knew it. That son of a bitch."

She sighed a little.

"When you told him about the baby, he accused you of trying to trap him into marriage, didn't he?"

Well, she could lie to her uncle or she could tell the truth and confirm his opinion of Mike. Jenny thought about it for a second, then decided she didn't need to protect her baby's father. "Yes, he did."

"Still thinks you're trying to wangle a deal for Snyder Arts?"

"I guess," she said on a sigh.

"Idiot," Hank muttered.

Before he could get going again, Jenny started talking. She wanted to say something that she should have said years ago. "Uncle Hank…"

The tone in her voice must have alerted him to a change in subject. He looked at her, concern shining in his eyes. "What is it?"

Lamps on the tables tossed golden light around the room. Outside, lights in homes and boats flickered in the darkness. This was home. Had been since she was a girl. And the comfort she felt here was something she was still grateful for.

She smiled a little. "I wanted to tell you something. When I first realized I was pregnant, I thought about all the responsibilities lying ahead. And I understood how you must have felt when my parents foisted me off on you."

"When they—"

"I just want you to know that I don't blame you for not wanting me, back then. I mean," she hurried on as Hank's forehead furrowed and his eyes narrowed, "I was twelve and you were alone and had your life and I was a—"

"Gift," Hank finished for her while she searched for the right word. "You were a gift," he repeated as if making sure she understood exactly how he felt. "My sister and her husband were fools then and they're fools now—wherever they are. They didn't know what they had in you."

Stunned silent, Jenny could only watch him as he approached and cupped her face in his big hands.

"You opened up my life, Jenny. Of course I wanted you. You're my family. You've been a joy, always. You're my *daughter* more than my niece. And now, you've given an old man something to look forward to—you're going to make me a grandfather."

Her vision blurry from behind a sheen of tears, Jenny could only look up at the one steady presence she'd known her whole life.

"No more of this not-wanting-you stuff, okay?" he asked. "Don't you ever even think it. Understand?"

She nodded because she didn't trust herself to speak. Her heart was too full to allow for mere words to explain what she felt.

"Good," he said with a sharp nod. "We've got that settled once and for all. But as for Mike Ryan…"

"Uncle Hank, this isn't all on Mike. I'm a big girl—"

"You're too trusting and he's a man used to taking what he wants. That's the issue here," Hank muttered darkly. He paced again as if he couldn't stand still another minute. "Thinks because he's richer than Croesus he can just call the tune everyone's supposed to dance to."

Jenny rolled her eyes and he saw that, too.

"I'm wound up and I know it," he said, "but with reason."

"I appreciate it, really I do," Jenny told him and

walked across the comfortably furnished and oh-so-familiar room to his side.

Nothing in this house had changed in decades. There were comfy chairs, heavy tables and a stone-faced fireplace. The cream-colored walls were covered with paintings by local artists—and a few of Jenny's early works. He had a housekeeper who'd been with him for thirty years and ran the house like a general his battalion.

"You're going to have the man's baby, Jenny. He should offer to marry you. It's what's right—not that Mike Ryan would know that."

She blew out a breath as she looked into the older man's worried eyes. Uncle Hank was tall and lanky, with thick gray hair, steely blue eyes and a stubborn jaw that was now set as if he were ready to bite through a box of nails. He had been the one steady influence in her life and he was the only family she really had. Her parents had disappeared from her life so many years ago, Jenny had no idea if they were living or dead. Hank, though, had always been there for her.

Even though, despite what he had just said, she couldn't imagine it had been easy for him to take on a twelve-year-old girl out of the blue.

She had known even then that she was his duty. She hadn't believed he'd really wanted her—why would he? His life was simple, uncomplicated. Why would he take on a twelve-year-old with abandonment issues voluntarily? But he'd taken her in, cared for her, seen her through school and dating, and even hired Jenny for her first real job as a summer intern at Snyder Arts. Hank had been the one to give her pastels and inks and sketch pads. He'd seen her raw talent and encouraged her to grow it. She would always owe him for that and for so much more.

"I don't need him to marry me," she said softly, laying one hand on her uncle's arm.

"'Course you don't, but he should have offered, damn it, not made you feel like a cheat or worse."

"I don't want a man who's forced to marry me because of circumstances." She remembered the look on Mike's face before he left. The harsh words they'd thrown at each other, and though it tore at her to admit it, Jenny knew that it was over between them. A low, throbbing ache settled into her heart and she had the distinct feeling that it would be there with her forever.

"So you'd have said no if he'd asked?"

"Yes," she said and knew he didn't really understand. In Hank's world, a man took care of his responsibilities. But what he didn't get was that Jenny didn't want to be the duty Mike picked up and carried under duress. If he didn't love her and want her, she didn't want him, either.

She still loved him, though, damn it. Even hearing his accusations hadn't been enough to kill off her feelings. Did that make her crazy or just stupid? She didn't know. All Jenny could hope was that the love she felt for Mike would slowly fade away.

Besides, she hadn't really been surprised when Mike didn't want her. No one ever really had. Until today, she would have said that not even her uncle had wanted her.

And she would never allow her child to feel that way.

"Mike Ryan." Hank shook his head and gray hair sproinged out around his head until he looked like a taller, more handsome Albert Einstein. "What were you thinking, honey? You know that man isn't to be trusted."

"Funny," she mused. "He says the same about *me*."

Hank stabbed his index finger toward her. "That tells you everything you need to know about the man. You're the most honest person I've ever known. If he can't see that, it's a lack in him, not you."

Warmth trickled through her. "Thanks, Uncle Hank."

"You don't have to thank me for the truth, honey," he said, shoving both hands into his pockets. "And I'm sorry to be carrying on so, but it just pops my corn that the man has taken advantage of you this way."

Jenny's mouth quirked. He sounded as if he thought she was a vestal virgin tempted out of her temple by Blackbeard.

"Uncle Hank…"

"Fine, fine." He lifted both hands. "You're a grown woman and you don't need your old uncle spouting off when you've got plenty to think about on your own."

"Thank you, though," she said, putting her arms around his waist. "For the outrage. For the support. For loving me."

True to form, Hank stiffened a little, as he always had. Hugs seemed to flummox him a bit, as if he wasn't quite sure what to do in response. And Jenny had often wondered what his late wife had been like. If she'd lived, would he be more comfortable with displays of emotion? He gave her a few awkward pats on her shoulder, then eased her back so he could look into her eyes.

"Are you all right with this?" he wanted to know. "I mean, you're healthy? You're going to be okay?"

"I'm fine and yes, I'm going to be great." She smiled. "I want this baby, Uncle Hank."

"Then I'll do whatever I can to help you, honey."

She smiled again. Hank wasn't the most outwardly

affectionate man, but he was loyal and kind and depend-
able. If he made a promise, he kept it.

"What're you going to do about your job?" he asked.

"To tell you the truth, I don't know." She bit at her
bottom lip as she thought about it. "Working with Mike
for months will be impossible now. Especially once word
gets out around the office—and it will—that I'm carrying his child."

Hank frowned and looked as though he wanted to
say something else, but he kept his silence and Jenny
went on.

"But I'm not going to do anything about it right now.
I've got the hotel in Nevada to finish."

"You're still going to do it?"

"Absolutely," she told him. Not only was she too
invested in the project to give it up now, but being in
Laughlin working would keep her from having to deal
with Mike every day. "It's a fabulous opportunity and I
don't want to give it up. I've got the whole thing planned
out and letting someone else take it over is just impossible."

"Always were stubborn," he muttered.

"Wonder where I got it," she countered and went up
on her toes to kiss his cheek.

He looked pleased but baffled.

"Come on in and eat, you two. Dinner's going cold
on the table."

Jenny looked over at Betty Sanders, housekeeper,
cook and, as Uncle Hank liked to call her, his nemesis.
She was short and thin, disproving the theory that a great
cook had to be big. She wore jeans and a sweatshirt and
had her long gray hair in a braid wrapped around the
back of her head like a halo.

Jenny appreciated the offer, but she wasn't all that hungry, either. "Thanks, Betty, but—"

"If you're going to have a baby, you're going to feed it. Now come in and sit down." Betty had helped raise Jenny and had run Hank's house and life for too long to stop now.

"Might as well," Uncle Hank said with a shrug. "You know she won't quit hounding you until you do."

"True." Jenny walked with him into the dining room, glad to be here in the home she'd loved growing up. Out the windows was a view of Balboa Bay, with beautiful houses lined along the shore and boats tied up at the docks.

When she first came here, Jenny had spent a lot of time down on the dock, watching the boats sail past, wondering if her parents would come back, if Hank would send her somewhere else. She'd felt lost and alone until the day her uncle had come out, sat down beside her and said, *If you're going to be spending so much time out on the dock, I'd better teach you how to sail.*

He took her out on his boat that very afternoon and for the first time in her life, she'd felt the amazing freedom in skimming across the water's surface, feeling the wind stream through her hair. He'd let her steer the boat, putting his big hands over hers on the wheel and explaining the harbor and the neighborhood that was now hers. That's when she'd understood that she was there to stay. Hank had given her everything in that one afternoon.

At the round oak table in the dining room, all three of them sat down and dug into the hearty bowls of homemade potato soup. While they ate, they talked, and Jenny was glad her uncle seemed to be calming down.

"There's just no point in worrying over what is," Betty

said, with a warning look at Hank. "Jenny's fine and she'll keep being fine with or without a man."

"'Course she will," Uncle Hank shot back. "That's not the point."

"It's exactly the point," Betty argued. "Why would you want her to have a man who doesn't really see her for who she is?"

"I want him to do the right thing, is all."

"The right thing is to walk away if you can't care."

Jenny felt as if she were at a tennis match. Her head swiveled back and forth as she followed the heated conversation that swirled around her as if she wasn't even there. Through the windows, she could see tiny white patio lights strung across the pergola, blinking like fireflies.

"I'm just saying she shouldn't have to do all of this alone," Uncle Hank muttered with a nodding glance at Jenny.

"She's not going to be alone," Betty snapped. "She's got us, doesn't she? We don't count?"

Jenny smiled, reached out and covered Betty's hand with her own. Betty was right. She wasn't alone. She had family. A family that Uncle Hank had given her. She grabbed for her uncle's hand, too, linking the three of them.

"She's right, you know," Uncle Hank told her, with just a touch of discomfort. "You've got us. For whatever you need."

"Thank you," she said, as warmth spread through her. He'd given her a real gift today. He'd let her know that her early fears in childhood hadn't had a basis in reality. He had wanted her. Still did. And now, he was making another choice, Jenny thought. A deliberate one, to once again be there—not just for her, but for her baby.

"Jenny," Betty said, giving her hand a quick pat, "you should think about moving back home."

"What?"

"That's a good idea," Uncle Hank piped up. "Never did like the idea of you living alone."

"Nonsense, why shouldn't she live alone?" Betty countered. "You're living in the dark ages, Hank. What I'm saying is, with a baby coming, she should come back home where she will have all the help she needs."

Both of them turned to look at Jenny, waiting for her response. Though she really appreciated the thought, Jenny wasn't ready to give up her little apartment and go running back home. Maybe that would change later on, when the baby's due date was closer, when she began to worry about being able to handle everything on her own.

But for now... "Thanks," she said, meaning it completely. "I appreciate that a lot, really." She looked from one to the other of them. "But I'm fine for now. I have my work and my own space."

Betty and Hank exchanged a knowing look, then her uncle turned to her. "Okay, but..." He paused and with an embarrassed shrug added, "You should remember that you've got a home here. People ready to help."

Jenny's eyes filled with tears but she blinked them back because she knew if she cried, Uncle Hank would panic. Instead, she squeezed his hand and whispered, "Thank you, Uncle Hank."

He squeezed back briefly. "No need to thank family."

Betty gave a loud sniffle, then snapped, "All right, now, that's enough of that. Soup's getting cold and, Jenny, you need to eat. That baby doesn't need a skinny mama."

Smiling to herself, Jenny did as she was told.

* * *

Mike spent the next few days at home. He couldn't go to the office because there, he'd have to deal with Jenny and he needed some damn time to come to grips with what had happened.

A baby.

Because of faulty condoms, he was going to be a father and he couldn't quite wrap his head around that one simple fact. Mike had never considered having children. To his mind, being a father meant being married and he'd never do that. Never give another person the ability to cut him off at the knees. To bring misery and—

Hell.

He left the silence of the house and stalked across the stone patio that led down a wide sweep of lawn toward the cliff. Beyond those cliffs was the Pacific and as he stared out at the ocean, glittering brightly beneath the morning sun, he squinted to see the handful of sailboats skimming the water. Closer to shore, there were a few surfers waiting for a decent wave.

The sound of the ocean reached him and the steady pulse of water against rocks seemed to steady him. He'd bought this house mainly for the view. It was too damn big for a man alone and he knew it, but until today, the quiet and the…emptiness really hadn't bothered him much.

Now, though, he looked at the pristine backyard and pictured a swing set there. He turned and stared at the shining windows and imagined Jenny in one of them, smiling down at him as she held their child in her arms.

Shaking his head, he rubbed his eyes and told himself he was just tired. Not surprising since he hadn't gotten much sleep over the past few days. How could he when memories of Jenny kept intruding? He saw her as she was the night he'd come to her after a miserable dinner at his parents' house. In her flannel pajama bottoms and slinky tank top. Saw her eyes as she leaned into his kiss. Heard her sighs as he entered her.

"How the hell is a man supposed to sleep when his own mind is working against him?" he demanded of no one.

"It's a bad sign when you talk to yourself."

Mike spun around to see Sean strolling out of the house and down the patio toward him. "When did you get back?"

"Last night," Sean said, shaking his head. "It was a hell of a storm. Kept us locked down for way too long." He tipped his head back, stared up at the blue, sunny sky and sighed. "It's good to be back in the sun. Man, I thought I'd never get warm again."

Mike gave him a halfhearted smile. It shamed him to realize he hadn't given Sean a thought in days. His own brother trapped in a snowstorm and he hadn't wondered once how he was doing. But now, it was good to steer his brain in a different direction. "You didn't kill the contractor, did you?"

Sean shot him a look, frowned and said, "No. Didn't kill her."

Mike frowned, too. "Something going on there?"

"Not a damn thing," Sean told him, then changed the subject abruptly. "I don't want to talk about Kate Wells, all right? Went by the office this morning. Glad to see everyone got the final changes in on 'The Wild Hunt.'"

Huffing out a breath, Mike realized he hadn't paid attention to that, either. One of their biggest games getting ready to roll onto the assembly line and he hadn't bothered to dot the i's and cross the t's.

"Jenny's Wise Woman character turned out spectacularly. Dave showed me the final sketches. That woman is talented."

"Yeah." Mike turned his face into the wind. Jenny was talented. And beautiful. And exasperating. And *pregnant*.

Sean was still talking. "Linda told me you haven't been in to the office in days. You sick or something?"

"Or something," Mike said. "You want some coffee?"

"Got a cappuccino on the way over." Sean grinned. "It was worth waiting for. But you're stalling. What's going on, Mike?"

He shoved his hands into the back pockets of his faded jeans and rocked on his heels. He hadn't told anyone about Jenny. About the baby. If Brady had been here, instead of in Ireland, Mike might have spilled the whole thing. But now, Sean was here and he found he needed to say it all out loud.

"It's Jenny," he said, looking at his brother. "She's pregnant."

A second or two ticked past as Sean simply stared at him, a befuddled expression on his face. Then a slow smile curved his mouth and he said, "I *knew* there was something going on between you two. And there's a baby? That's great, right?" He rushed across the patio and gave his brother a brief, hard hug. "I like Jenny a lot," he said, stepping back and grinning. "And everybody's noticed the red-hot chemistry between you two."

Mike went still. He'd been sure that what was between Jenny and him was a secret. Private. "Everybody noticed? You mean people at work know about—"

"Well, they don't *know*, but sure, there's been some talk." Sean shrugged. "Mostly the women. They really notice the stuff that sails right over most guys' heads."

"Great. That's great." Just what he wanted. All of his employees knowing about his private life, speculating, maybe even making bets on what would happen next.

"What's the problem?" Sean asked. "It's not like it would have stayed a secret for long. Not with Jenny pregnant. And here's another question. If she's pregnant, why is she out working on the hotel in Laughlin and you're not with her?"

"She's in Laughlin?"

"Yeah. Linda says she went out yesterday. She didn't want to take the jet, so she drove, hauling all of her paint supplies with her." He paused. "And you didn't know anything about this, did you?"

"No." Mike wasn't happy about it, either. She could have told him she was driving out alone to Laughlin. He thought about that long, lonely road through the desert. Hell, there were sections where you could go for *miles* with nothing but sand on either side of your car. "She didn't tell me."

"Why wouldn't she?"

Mike snapped his brother a hard look. "None of your business."

"What'd you do, Mike?"

"I didn't *do* anything," he argued, feeling defensive even though he knew there was no reason for it.

"Yeah? The woman you're crazy about is pregnant with your kid and you look like you want to punch somebody." Sean tipped his head to one side and said, "Why don't you spill what's really going on?"

"She did this on purpose," he muttered.

"Wow. She *forced* you to have sex with her?" Sean snorted. "You poor guy."

"Shut up, Sean."

"Do you get how ridiculous you sound? Get over yourself, Mike. She didn't trick you. Or trap you. Hell, you're not that great a prize."

"Thanks. So glad you're home." Mike scrubbed one hand across the back of his neck and remembered that Jenny had said the same damn thing to him not so long ago. But you'd think his own brother would be a little more supportive.

"Come on, Mike. Condoms leak. Nothing's perfect." Sean slapped Mike's shoulder. "So you gonna marry her or what?"

"No, I'm not marrying her."

"Why the hell not?" Sean threw both hands high, clearly exasperated. "She's gonna have your baby and you're obviously nuts about her."

"I need more coffee." Mike walked away from his brother to the glass-topped table at the edge of the patio. There, he poured a cup of coffee from the thermal hot pot his housekeeper had brought out. He took a sip and let the heat slide through him.

"What's going on?" Sean followed him. "I can't believe you won't marry her. This is your kid we're talking about, Mike. Marrying her is the right thing to do and you know it."

His head was pounding, brain racing. Sean's haranguing wasn't helping with the headache throbbing behind his eyes. He hadn't slept, hadn't been able to think clearly in days, and now he'd found out Jenny was in Laughlin— without bothering to tell him.

"What do you think Mom and Dad'll have to say when they find out?"

"They should understand better than anyone." Mike's gaze shot to his brother's and before he could stop himself, he was blurting out the secret he'd held since he was thirteen. "I'm not marrying anybody, you understand? I won't risk being lied to, cheated on. You think I want to take a chance on ruining my own kid's life?"

"What the hell are you talking about?"

Too late to pull it back now, Mike told his brother about the day his own image of the perfect family had been shattered. "When I was thirteen, I came home from baseball practice and found Mom crying," he said tightly. "I was worried, thought maybe Dad had been in an accident or something."

"What was it?"

He could still remember it all so clearly. Sunshine pouring through the kitchen window. His mom sitting at the table, head in her hands, crying. He'd never seen her cry before and it scared him.

Mike set his coffee cup down, crossed his arms over his chest and said, "She grabbed me into a hard hug and she told me that Dad had cheated on her. That she found out he'd been out with some woman."

"No way." Sean's eyes went hard and cool and flat.

Mike knew how he felt. Back then, it had seemed to Mike as though the floor had opened up beneath him. He'd worried about his mom, wondered if his dad would ever come home again. Would they get a divorce? Who would he live with? A thirteen-year-old kid shouldn't have to think about any of it. Shouldn't have to learn so suddenly that his parents were flawed. Human.

"She never would have let any of it slip if I hadn't

caught her in a vulnerable moment," he said, and knew it for truth since his mom had apologized over and over again over the years. "Dad lied. To her. To us. He was a liar and a cheat and ever since that day, I can't be around him without remembering our mother crying."

Sean looked away toward the ocean and Mike finished. "I won't get married, Sean. I won't put my faith in someone only to be lied to and cheated on. Not gonna happen. I won't risk my kid being destroyed by lies."

After a moment or two, Sean turned his head to look at him and Mike read the fury in his brother's eyes.

"You had no right," Sean said tightly. "No right to keep this from me. I'm a Ryan, too."

"Why the hell should you feel as crappy as me?" Mike argued. "You didn't have to know and a lot of the time I wished to hell I didn't know."

"And you make the choice for me, is that it? You decide what I should know, what I should think?"

"That's not it," Mike said.

"Sure it is," Sean snapped. "You don't even see it, do you? You've been mad at Dad for years for lying. Every time you talk about Jenny, you call her a liar, say you can't trust her. But you've been lying to me since we were kids.

"So what's the difference, Mike? Are you the only one who gets to lie? Do you get to decide which is a good lie and which is bad?"

Mike had never thought about it exactly like that until now and he didn't know what he could say to the accusation. His father's lies had destroyed Mike's image of a happy family. Mike's own lies of omission were to protect Sean from the same hurt Mike felt.

And yet today, Sean was slapped with not one, but two sets of lies.

"You ought to take a good look at yourself, big brother," Sean said quietly. "Whatever was between our parents back then? They fixed it. Healed it. In case you hadn't noticed, they're still together, stronger than ever."

Truth could hit as hard as lies.

"So don't kid yourself. This isn't about Dad. Or Jenny. This is all on you, Mike. You're the liar now." Sean turned and walked away, stalking across the patio and into the house.

Alone in the yard, Mike felt the ground he'd built his life on tremble beneath his feet. Sean was right, he realized. Which meant that Mike was wrong. About a lot of things.

Nine

Laughlin in February was pretty.

The summer heat was still a few months off and the river was quiet but for the inevitable tour boats and an occasional Jet Ski. There were a lot of snowbirds in town, older people coming in to escape snow country with a few months in the desert. Tourists were always there of course, and every day, pontoon boats full of visitors to the city slowed to watch the progress being made on the River Haunt.

True to his word, the contractor, Jacob Schmitt, was keeping to schedule. He had men working on both the hotel facade and the interior, where Jenny spent most of her time. There was the constant drone of saws and the slamming of hammers, not to mention shouted conversations and laughter ringing out all around her.

But she was still glad she'd come. Being in the desert, away from the office for a while, had been a great idea. In Nevada, she didn't have to deal with the worry of having to face Mike again so soon after their confrontation. It hurt, knowing that their connection was over. But it would be even more painful if she had to see him every day. To be reminded of what they might have had.

No, what she needed was a little space, a little time, to get used to the idea that she was going to be a single mother.

She'd always wanted to have kids—lots of them. But in her secret dreams, she also had a husband who loved her. That little dream wasn't going to come true, though. Remembering the look on Mike's face when she told him she was pregnant was enough to convince her of that. Even if she didn't also have the memory of him accusing her of trying to trap him into marriage.

Pain and anger twisted into a knot that sat like lead in the pit of her stomach.

"He really is an idiot," she muttered, swiping a paintbrush loaded with deep violet paint across the entryway wall. Why couldn't she have fallen in love with someone—*anyone*—else? Why did Mike Ryan have to be the only man for her?

Jenny sighed and finished covering the wall with the paint she'd chosen for the biggest impact. Once it was dry she'd lay out the lines for the forest, the moon and the hints of figures she wanted lost in the trees. It would take a few days, but that was okay with her.

She had driven out here with a plan to stay for at least a week. Heaven knew there were plenty of hotel rooms to choose from and she wouldn't be lonely, either. Not with the security people and the hotel employees staying here, as well.

Besides, being on-site, she could oversee the other artists she'd hired to help with the murals. There were three of them, all talented, but artists were temperamental people and just as likely to go off plan and add their own visions to a design. But that couldn't happen here. The designs had all been approved by Mike, Sean and Brady already, so there was no deviating from them.

"Hey, Jenny!"

She looked up at the friendly shout. Tim Ryerson, one of the hotel employees, stood at the front door. "What's up, Tim?"

"Some of us are going into town for lunch. You up for it?"

They were all being so nice to her, but what Jenny really wanted was quiet and some time to herself. "Thanks, but I think I'll stay here and get started on the dining room mural."

"You're allowed to have fun, too, you know," he said with a sad shake of his head.

"Thanks, but for me, this *is* fun."

"Okay, then." He shrugged good-naturedly. "Can we bring you back anything?"

"A burger," she said quickly. "And lots of fries."

She was starting to get her appetite back—at least in the afternoons—and she wasn't sure if that was a good thing or not. She was so short that if she kept eating like this, by the time the baby was born, she'd look like a soccer ball.

"You got it. Later."

Once he and the others had gone, the hotel fell into blessed quiet. Lunchtime was the one time of the day she could count on a little peace. Even the crew's ever-playing radio was silent as the men left to get something to eat. She had the place to herself for the next hour and Jenny relished it.

Leaving the main wall to dry, she walked into the dining room and studied the long partition that separated the room from the kitchen. She'd have Tony and Lena work this wall, setting out the characters and scenery from the "River Haunt" game that would bring the room to life. Christa could work on the vines that would trail around the windows at the front of the room. If they all worked together, they could knock this out in a few days and move upstairs to the hallways. According to the plans, there would be vines, flowers and a banshee or two in each of the long halls, and haunting trees, bent in an invisible wind, painted on to the elevator doors.

She looked around the dining room and saw it as it would be when finished. As in the castle in Ireland, this dining hall would consist of long, banquet-style tables and benches, forcing guests to intermingle during meals. The gamers who came here would huddle together, talking scores and routes and walk-throughs of the game itself.

Guests who were unfamiliar with the game would soon be drawn into the fantasy world of Celtic Knot and the plush environment of the hotel. Once again, Jenny was impressed by the foresight of the Ryans and Brady Finn. By expanding their company into other realms, they were going to build the brand that was already becoming known around the world. To have a small part in this expansion was both exhilarating and sad. Because she knew without a doubt that this project would be one of her last for Celtic Knot.

In the quiet, her mind drifted to thoughts of Mike and she wondered what he was doing. If he even knew she was gone. And if he would care. If only he'd trusted her. Believed in her. Her heart ached when she remembered the expression on his face when he learned about the baby.

He'd come to her concerned that she wasn't feeling well and then left her, convinced that she was trying to use him. How could it all turn so bad so quickly? Why couldn't he see that she loved him? That if given the chance, the two of them and their child could have something wonderful? Was he so hard, so accustomed to shutting down his heart to keep possible pain at bay that he couldn't risk it for a chance for happiness?

Her own pain blossomed in her chest until it squeezed her heart and she had to force herself to stop thinking of what-ifs and of Mike, because there was no help there. Nothing was going to change and it was best if she got used to that as soon as possible.

Patting her belly, Jenny whispered, "Don't worry, baby. We're going to be okay. You'll see." She got back to work, pushing thoughts of Mike and her up-in-the-air life to the back of her mind. Time enough to worry when she was lying awake all night.

Mike almost called Jenny. Twice. And each time, he hung up before the call could connect. He was still on edge after having Sean ream him, so it probably wasn't the best time to talk to her anyway. But she was there. In his thoughts. In his soul.

She was off in the desert and hadn't bothered to tell him. Because when she told him about the baby, he'd turned on her.

That shamed him, but now, with Sean's temper still burning his ears, Mike admitted that it was past time to settle a few things that had been guiding him for years. He drove to his parents' house, determined to finally talk to his mother about what had happened so long ago. To figure out if that one day, that one secret, was worth steering his entire life by.

The house looked the same as it always had. No matter how successful he and his brother had become, Jack and Peggy Ryan hadn't allowed their sons to buy them a bigger place in a more upscale neighborhood. They preferred staying in the house where they'd raised their family, where they knew their neighbors and where every room held a memory. On this familiar street, houses were well cared for, yards were neat and nearly every driveway sported a basketball hoop.

Mike parked the car, then let himself in the front door, yelling to announce his presence. "Hey, Mom! It's me!"

The house was quiet but for the low murmur of the television, set to a 1960s music channel. He walked through the living room, past the neat kitchen and into the den, and still didn't find her. "Mom?"

"Mike, is that you?"

Relief shot through him as he turned to watch her approach. Her light brown hair was in a tangle and she was tugging at the hem of a pale pink shirt.

"You okay?" he asked, since she looked harried and a little nervous.

"Fine. You just caught me in the middle of something." Then his mother *blushed*.

Mike suddenly had the feeling that he'd walked in on something he'd rather not think about. "Look, I'll come back another time and—"

"Don't be silly," his mother said, already walking.

"Come into the kitchen. There's coffee and I made cookies this morning."

If she was willing to pretend she hadn't blushed, Mike could do it, too. "Sold."

"Good, good," she said, smiling now as she smoothed her hair. "Come and tell me why you stopped by. Is everything all right?"

"That's a good question."

"Sit down," she ordered when they were in the bright, sunny yellow kitchen. She poured coffee, set it in front of him, then brought a plate of cookies to the table, as well. Holding a cup of coffee, she sat down opposite him and said simply, "Tell me."

How many times over the years had he sat at this table with a plate of cookies in front of him and his mother listening to whatever problem he'd brought her? It was at this table where he'd found her crying. Where his life had taken that abrupt turn from innocence into suspicion. It was only fitting, he supposed, to be sitting at this table again while making the attempt to turn back.

So he told her about Jenny, about the baby, about Sean now knowing what happened all those years ago and how pissed his little brother was to find out he'd been lied to for years.

"What about Jenny?" his mother asked. "She's pregnant with your child. Do you love her?"

Mike shook his head. Of course she would zero in on that part of the story. "Another good question."

He pushed up from the table, walked to the counter, then turned around, bracing both hands on the granite countertop behind him. "But for right now, that doesn't even matter."

"Michael Patrick Ryan," his mother said, drawing a reflexive wince from her son, "love is *all* that matters."

"How can you say that, Mom, when—" He shook his head. "When you were cheated on. Lied to."

"That's it. I've had enough." Peggy stood up, pointed at the kitchen table and ordered, "Sit down. I'll be right back."

He did as instructed mainly because he was too tired to keep standing. If he didn't get some sleep soon, he'd go through life a zombie.

When his mother came back, she was dragging his father with her. Jack's hair was messy and he was trying to button his shirt as he was pulled in his wife's wake. And suddenly, Mike knew exactly what his parents had been doing when he dropped by. And yeah, he'd rather not think about that. Didn't matter how old you got, nobody wanted to imagine their parents having sex.

Mike stiffened and he noticed that Jack Ryan did the same. His father was an older version of himself, with sharp blue eyes, and a sprinkling of gray at his temples. The two of them were still so uncomfortable with each other over something that had happened twenty years before. But damned if Mike knew how to get past it, get over it.

"Both of you sit down right now," Peggy said and crossed her arms over her chest until her men complied. Then she looked from her husband to her son before saying softly, "Mike, I've tried to talk to you about this before, but you never wanted to listen. I could have *made* you hear me out, but your father wouldn't allow that." She spared Jack a glance and a smile. "He wanted you to come to us yourself when you were ready. Frankly, I thought it would never happen."

"Mom…"

"I never should have burdened you with what I felt that day," Peggy said. "But you came home early from practice and found me, crying, and somehow it all came out. And I hope you know that if I could wipe it from your mind, I would."

"I know all that, Mom—" He shot a look at his father, who looked every bit as uncomfortable as he felt. "We don't have to talk about it again."

"That's the problem," Peggy said, pulling out a chair and taking a cookie that she began to crumble between her fingers. "We've never talked about it." Her gaze softened as she looked at Mike. Then she took her husband's hand and threaded her fingers through his. "Mike, you were just a little boy, so you don't remember, but back then, your dad's business was in trouble."

Jack picked up the thread and Mike looked at his father as he spoke. "It's not an excuse but we were under a lot of pressure and instead of talking to each other about it—" he paused and smiled sadly at his wife "—we each closed down, shut each other out."

"We were wrong. We handled it all badly. But it takes two to make or break a marriage, Mike. So you were wrong to blame only your father all these years. We both made mistakes. We both nearly lost something most people never find."

Mike heard them, saw how together they were on this, but he couldn't let go. Turning to face his father, he said quietly, "You lied. You cheated."

"I did lie," Jack said. "I was hurt, worried about my family. Feeling like a damn failure and as if I were alone in the mess and missing your mother because we weren't talking to each other anymore."

"Oh, Jack…"

He squeezed her hand and then looked at Mike again. "I did lie, I give you that. And I cheated, too, I guess, but not the way you mean."

"What?"

Jack sighed. "The woman your mother heard about— I did take her to dinner. We talked. She listened to me, laughed at my jokes, made me feel important." He shook his head. "Stupid. It was stupid, but I didn't sleep with her, Mike." Jack's gaze met his son's squarely. "I never touched another woman from the day I married your mother."

Peggy spoke up then. "Instead of being there for each other, your dad and I pulled apart until we were each so far from the other, it was as if we were two strangers living in this house together."

Jack lifted their joined hands and kissed her knuckles. "What's important is that we found each other again before it was too late."

"I don't even know what to say," Mike muttered. For twenty years, he and his father had sidestepped each other, neither of them willing to talk about the thing that had put a wedge between them.

"Why didn't you tell me?" he asked.

"Because you wouldn't have believed me," Jack said.

"I guess that's true enough," Mike admitted. So much time being angry, letting old pains rule his life, believing that no one could be trusted because he had looked at a situation he didn't understand through the eyes of a wounded thirteen-year-old boy.

"The point is, honey," Peggy said, "you've been using your father as an excuse to keep everyone at a distance. You're protecting yourself from being hurt by not letting anything at all touch you." She shook her head. "That's no way to live, sweetie."

She was right, Mike thought. He had been using his father's betrayal as a way to keep everything and everyone else at a distance. And even with the walls he'd erected around his heart, Jenny had found a way in.

"You never should have been aware of that bump in our marriage," Peggy said. "And it breaks my heart to see the two of you so far apart."

Mike looked to his father and in the older man's eyes, he saw the same sorrow, the same sense of loss that Mike had felt for years. Now he was forced to do some serious thinking. Sean's words still echoed in his head as he thought back on all the years of sitting in a position of judgment, so sure he was right and everyone else was wrong. He had shut down emotionally. At the ripe old age of thirteen, not knowing anything at all about the world or what adults had to do to survive, he'd made a decision that had affected his entire life.

He had been a kid making a child's decisions, and he had allowed those decisions to rule him. If he'd once come down off his throne of righteousness and actually *talked* to the people around him, maybe this tightness around his heart could have been eased years ago.

"What happened wasn't your fault," his father said carefully. "You were a boy and you reacted how you had to at the time."

"Yeah," Mike said, rubbing his eyes to ease the throbbing headache settled behind them. "But I never let go of that decision. An angry, scared, thirteen-year-old boy chose that day to believe that no one could be trusted."

His father reached out and laid one hand on Mike's shoulder, and the heavy, solid strength of that touch seemed to ease away the last of that long-ago boy's resolve. He looked at his dad and said simply, "I'm sorry."

"You don't have to be," Jack told him. "Parents aren't supposed to give their kids burdens to carry. And I did that to you. I hurt you, your mother, all of us. It's something I'll never forgive myself for."

Peggy sniffled and swiped tears off her cheeks. "It's been long enough, hasn't it?" she asked. "Can we all let it go now and be the family we should be?"

Mike looked at his mother, still holding her husband's hand as she watched her oldest son with worry and hope at war in her eyes. The old hurts and fears and convictions dropped away, slipping into the past where they belonged, and Mike let them go. He felt as if a weight had been lifted from him and it surprised him to realize just how heavy that burden had been.

"Yeah," he said, smiling first at his mother and then at his father. "I'd like that."

Jack grinned, slapped Mike's shoulder again and then looked at his wife. Peggy gave him a watery smile in return then reached for her son's hand and held it tightly. "Good. This is good."

She was right about that. It was good, to get past pain and anger and betrayal. But his father wasn't the only one he'd judged. Mike thought back to that night in Phoenix when he'd spotted a beautiful blonde in a conference hotel bar. He remembered the rush, the pull toward her, and he remembered the next morning when he'd become judge, jury and executioner without once giving her a chance to explain.

Then those memories morphed into his last image of Jenny, at her house when he accused her of trying to trap him into marriage. He'd done the same damn thing to her all over again.

"Sean's right," he muttered. "I am an idiot."

"What's wrong, honey?"

He lifted his gaze to his mother's and sighed. "A lot. I've got some thinking to do. About Jenny. The baby." He stopped, smiled. "And you guys will have to get used to the idea of being grandparents."

"Oh, my goodness," Peggy exclaimed with a laugh. "With all the tumult I almost forgot that Jenny's pregnant!"

"Grandfather?" Jack asked.

"This is wonderful news!" Peggy jumped to her feet and wagged her finger at her son. "I'm making a fresh pot of coffee and you, mister, are going to tell us everything."

Jack picked up a cookie and handed it to him. "Congratulations. I hope you do a better job of it than I did."

Mike shook his head and took a bite of the cookie. He'd already made mistakes and his child wasn't even born yet. "You didn't do so badly, Dad. But for me, I swear I don't know what the hell I'm doing."

Jack laughed. "Welcome to parenthood. None of us know what we're doing, Mike. And even trying our very best, we all make mistakes. The trick is to keep trying to fix them."

Mike found Sean in his office the next morning. He'd thought about this all night, had worked out just what he wanted to say. But looking into his brother's unforgiving stare threw him for a second. The two of them had always been close, but now, there was a wedge between them that Mike himself had put there. So it was up to him to tear it out.

"You were right."

Surprised, Sean waved him to a chair. "Always a good start to a conversation. Continue."

Mike laughed and sat down. "I've been protecting you since we were kids," he said thoughtfully. He'd had all night to consider this situation from every angle. And no matter how he looked at it, he came off badly. That didn't sit well with him. "It got to be a habit."

"Okay," Sean said, acknowledging that with a nod.

"But it was wrong to lie to you all those years." Mike sighed, leaned forward and braced his forearms on his thighs. "Whenever you asked me what was wrong between me and Dad, I brushed it off. Covered it up, telling myself you were better off not knowing. So, yeah. I made that call and I shouldn't have. You've been grown-up a long time, Sean, so shutting you out was the wrong call, but you should understand why I did it."

"You're really not very good at apologies, are you?"

Grumbling, Mike admitted, "No."

"Well, points for effort anyway," Sean said.

"Thanks." Mike nodded and told him, "I stopped by the house yesterday. Saw Mom and Dad. We talked."

"And...?"

"And," Mike said with a rueful smile on his face, "I apparently interrupted an afternoon quickie."

"Oh, man!" Laughing, Sean covered his eyes with one hand. "I didn't need to know that."

"Hey, you're the one who doesn't want me lying to him."

"Discretion, man. There's a difference between lies and discretion. Look it up."

Glad things were smoothed out between his brother and him, Mike chuckled. "The point is, we finally straightened everything out. I think things will be all right now, between me and Dad."

"Good to hear." Sean sat forward, folded his hands on the desktop.

"They know you know," Mike said. "I told them that I talked to you about it."

"Great. When you decide to be honest, you go all out, don't you?" A half smile curved Sean's mouth. "Guess I'll be having a talk with them, too, now. But as long as they're good together, happy together, I'm fine with it. It's all their business, Mike. Not mine. Not yours."

"When did you get so rational?"

"When I grew up," his brother said. "You missed that, I think."

"Yeah, looks like." Mike frowned. "I think I missed a lot."

"Ah, now we get to the important part of the conversation. Jenny."

Shooting his brother a hard look, Mike said, "You'll butt out of what happens to our parents, but I'm fair game?"

"Hell, yes." Sean grinned. "So, have you talked to her?"

"No." He still hadn't called, because talking to her on the phone wouldn't be enough. He had to look into her eyes, read what she was thinking, feeling.

"Don't you think you should?" Sean asked. "She's pregnant with your baby."

"I don't need reminding," Mike said and hopped out of the chair. Walking to the wide window on the far wall, he looked out at the garden and didn't see a thing. How could he, when his mind was filled with images of Jenny.

"Maybe you do." Sean waited until his brother looked

at him again to continue. "You've been in charge of things so long, you've forgotten how to just be Mike."

"That's ridiculous."

"Is it? You talk to Jenny like she's your employee..."

"She is."

"She's more, too," Sean said. "And it's the *more* you're not getting. To get what you really want out of all of this, you're going to have to get humble."

Mike snorted. "And you think you know what I want?"

"Yep," Sean mused. "Don't you?"

Yeah, he did. He wanted Jenny. In his house. In his bed. He wanted to wake up in the morning reaching for her and have her curl up against him. But "humble" wasn't the way to get it.

"You can't just march up to Jenny and order her to forgive you," Sean said.

"It's the easiest way," Mike mumbled.

"Yeah, if you want to tick her off even more."

He might have a point, but Mike didn't want to think about it. "Can you handle things here at the office for a few days?"

"Sure," Sean said. "Why?"

"Because," Mike said, "I'm going to Laughlin."

"It's about time," Sean told him.

Early the next afternoon, Jenny stood back from the wall to take an objective look at the finished painting. It was just as she'd imagined it. Hints of danger hidden among the trees, moonlight filtering through the leaves to dapple on the overgrown ground. A river wound through the back of the painting like a silver snake, a moonlit, watery path that only the brave would dare follow. The painting was vaguely menacing and intriguing and set just the right mood for the River Haunt hotel.

The other artists were doing a great job on the murals and already the dining room motif was coming together. Another day or two and they could move upstairs. While the construction crew were mostly huddled in the kitchen finishing the cabinets and the new countertops, Jenny walked through the lobby into what used to be the lounge.

Here, the plan was to have clusters of furniture scattered throughout and several game-playing stations set up, with four-flat screen TVs that invited guests to dive into Celtic Knot games. There would be a bar on the far wall where a battered old piano now stood and one section of the room would be set up with wide tables so guests could also play the role-playing board games as well.

It was going to be a gamer's paradise, she told herself with a smile. And that wasn't even taking into account the midnight pontoon rides on the river, where animatronic banshees, ghouls and hunters would lunge from their hiding places onshore. It was all going to be amazing.

Jenny hated knowing that she'd have to quit her job at Celtic Knot. She enjoyed being a part of something so fresh and interesting and fun. But working with Mike now was just impossible. She couldn't see him every day and know she'd never have him. So she'd do her best on this project and then she'd walk away, head high. And one day, she promised herself, she'd come to the River Haunt hotel as a guest, just so she could see people enjoying what she'd helped to build.

Sighing, she stopped at the piano and idly stroked a few keys. She hadn't really played since she was a girl and Uncle Hank had paid for the lessons she'd wanted so badly. That phase had lasted more than a year, Jenny remembered, and then she had discovered art and playing the piano had taken a backseat.

For an old instrument, the piano had good tone and as her fingers moved over the keys in a familiar piece from her childhood, the music lifted into the stillness. She sat down on the bench, closed her eyes and let her troubled thoughts slide away as she listened only to the tune she created.

Mike found her there. A small woman with a halo of golden hair, sitting in a patch of sunlight, teasing beautiful music from a piano that looked as old as time.

His heart gave one quick jolt in his chest. Damn, he'd missed her. Everything in him was drawn to her. How had she become so important to him in so short a time? She was talented, brilliant, argumentative and beautiful, and he wanted her so badly he could hardly breathe. Now that he was here, with her, he wasn't about to wait another minute to touch her.

Wrapped up in the music that soared around her, she didn't hear him approach. When Mike laid both hands on her shoulders, she jumped, spinning around on the bench, eyes wide.

"You *scared* me."

He grinned at the glint in her eyes. He'd even missed her temper. "I didn't mean to sneak up on you, but with the music, you couldn't hear me. I didn't know you played piano."

"I told you before, there's a lot you don't know about me."

"Yeah, I guess you're right," he said, and pulled her

up from the scarred wooden bench. "But there's plenty I do know."

"Like what?" she asked, taking one short step backward.

"Like," he said, closing the gap between them, "you're so stubborn you're probably getting ready to quit your job at Celtic Knot."

Clearly surprised, she asked, "How did you know that?"

"Wasn't hard to figure out, Jenny. You think it'll be too hard for us to work together now."

"I'm right and you know it, Mike."

"No. You're not," he said, and watched hope bloom in her eyes. Sean had been wrong. All Mike had to do was lay out his plan and she'd see that it was the best thing for everyone. "I think we should work together and more. We both want our baby. We have great chemistry. Passion."

His hands came down on her shoulders and he drew her closer. Looking down into those blue eyes of hers, he said, "We forget about the past. Let it all go and just move on from here. We're going to get married, Jenny. It's the right thing to do. For all of us."

He waited, for her to smile at him, go up on her toes and kiss him. He wanted the taste of her in his mouth again. It had been days and he felt as if it had been years. All she had to do was say yes.

"No."

She was screwing up a perfectly good plan. Staring down at her, he blurted, "Why the hell not? You're pregnant, remember?"

She laughed shortly. "Yes, I remember. And I won't marry you because you don't love me. You don't trust me. Passion isn't enough to build a marriage on, Mike.

And I won't risk my baby's happiness on a marriage doomed to failure."

"It's not doomed."

"Without love it is," she said, shaking her head. Laying one hand on his forearm, Jenny continued. "It's *our* baby, Mike. I would never try to keep you from him. Or her. But I won't marry a man who doesn't trust me."

Then she kissed him.

And left.

Ten

Jenny had a stalker.

For the next few days, every time she turned around, Mike was there. He carried her paints and insisted on getting her a chair if she so much as yawned. Only that morning, when she climbed a step ladder to add a few silvery cobwebs to a naked tree on an elevator door, he'd snatched her off the darn thing and carried her to her room. In spite of her loud protests. The man had appointed himself her caretaker whether she wanted one or not. It was annoying and endearing at the same time.

She didn't want to get used to this kind of treatment, though. Firstly because she was perfectly healthy and able to take care of herself. But mainly because she knew it was all for show. He was trying to schmooze her into marrying him on his terms.

But she couldn't do it. Couldn't give up her fantasies of a loving husband and settle for a man who didn't trust her, didn't love her. Passion was a poor substitute for real love.

"Jen, what do you think of this?"

Jenny popped out of her thoughts and focused instead on the job at hand. "What've you got, Christa?"

The other artist was tall and thin, with black hair cut close to her scalp and a penchant for wearing eye-searing colors. She was also fast, talented and eager to please.

"I was thinking about adding in a few of the Death Flowers among the vines here at the windows."

"Death Flowers?" Jenny repeated with a smile.

Christa shrugged. "I admit, I love the 'River Haunt' game. I play it with my fiancé all the time."

"Do you win?"

"Not so far," she admitted, "but I keep trying. Anyway, you know the bloodred flowers that have fangs? I thought if it's okay with you, I'd add a few of them here on these vines. I mean, they're not on the original design so I wanted to run it by you before I did anything."

The dining room was nearly finished. The far wall was complete and the forest scene was spectacular. Though she'd had a few problems with one of the artists, she couldn't fault the work. Jenny looked up at what Christa had done so far. The vines were thick and lush, wrapped around the edges of the windows and down to the bottom of the wall where a few of them even pooled on the floor. "You've done a great job here, Christa."

"Thanks," she said, stepping back to check out her own work. "I'm really grateful for the opportunity."

Jenny looked up at her. As short as she was, she pretty much looked up at *everyone*. "The flowers are a fabulous idea. I love it."

Christa grinned.

"Use your own eye for placement. Seeing your work, I trust your judgment."

"That is so cool. Thank you, Jenny." Christa's features lit up in pleasure.

"You know, when this project's finished, if you're interested, I'll talk to Dave Cooper, he's the head of the graphic arts department for Celtic Knot. I'm sure he could use an artist like you." She paused. "If you're interested."

"Seriously? Interested?" Christa laughed, then scooped Jenny up for a tight hug. "That would be like my dream job."

When she was on her feet again, Jenny grinned at the other woman's enthusiasm. "You could probably work from here, but Dave might ask you to move to California."

"Not a problem," Christa swore, lifting one hand as if taking an oath.

"What about your fiancé? Would he be willing to move for your job?"

Christa smiled. "He loves me, so sure. Of course. Plus, he's a writer, so he can work anywhere."

"Then I'll talk to Dave and let you know what he says."

"Thank you, Jenny. I mean it. This is just the ultimate thing that could have happened."

"You're welcome. But for right now, concentrate on the Death Flowers."

"They'll be the most bloodthirsty blossoms in the universe when I'm done with them," Christa vowed, and immediately bent to her paint palette.

Sure what she was feeling was etched on her features, Jenny was grateful that the other woman had turned away. She heard Christa's words echoing in her mind. *He loves me. So sure. Of course.* Envy whipped through her like a lash, leaving a stinging pain behind. Christa was so certain of her fiancé. So confident in his love and support. And Jenny yearned to know what that feeling was like.

Sighing, she watched for a few minutes as Christa laid out quick sketches for placement of the flowers. It was nice to be able to help someone so talented. Someone who'd already proven herself to be a team player. Jenny was sure that Dave would jump at the chance to bring aboard such a skilled artist. Especially since he'd be needing someone to take Jenny's place once she turned in her resignation. Oh, that thought hurt. She loved her job. Loved being a part of the magic of imagination. But she had to give it up. For the sake of her own sanity.

Jenny left the main floor and took the stairs to the third. She couldn't take the elevators, since they were shut down temporarily so the paintings on the doors could be completed. Wanting to take a quick look at the hallway up here, Jenny walked slowly, checking the progress of the artwork.

On the third floor, there were werewolves sprinting along the wall, muscled bodies ripping through ribbons of fog as they gazed out at the hall as if staring at those who walked past. Jenny admired the art even as she shivered at the images. Not exactly the kind of thing designed to promote an easy night's sleep. But then again, the gamers who would flock to this hotel would love the imagery. Then they would slip into their hotel rooms and play the games on the top-of-the-line gaming systems.

She smiled to herself, then gave a quick glance to the antiqued brass wall sconces, shaped to give the illusion of torches. A dark blue carpet runner stretched the length of the hallway, covering the center of the wood-grain ceramic tiles. It was a good idea, she thought, for the flooring. Giving the feel of wood while offering the much-easier-to-care-for tile.

She headed back to the staircase and then walked down to the second floor to peek at what the other two artists were doing with the banshee/ghost halls. When she found them, the artists were in a heated discussion and didn't even notice her approach.

"The banshees all have white hair," Lena shouted. "Have you ever played the game?"

"I'm an artist, I don't waste my time playing video games," Tony argued. "And what difference does it make if a banshee has black hair? They're not *real*, you know."

"No," Jenny said loudly enough to interrupt their argument. "Banshees aren't real, but they are integral to the game you're supposed to be replicating here."

He sighed heavily, dramatically, as if to let her know how put-upon he was to be questioned by anyone about his artistic decisions. Jenny had known when she hired the man that he was going to be difficult. But the sad truth was, his talent had won him the job. She'd run out of names of local artists and had had to take a chance on him being willing to play by the rules stated. It looked as though she'd made a bad call.

"Artistically speaking, a black-haired banshee will pop more from the cream colored walls," he argued.

"You jerk," the other artist countered. "If you knew anything about shadows and highlighting, you'd know how to make that white hair stand out. It's supposed to be otherworldly, not like a photo shoot for a fashion magazine."

"What you know about art," he shouted, "could be printed on a business card with room left over for a Chinese menu."

"I know enough to do what I've been contracted to do," she said.

Jenny's head ached. They'd had the same problems with Tony while finishing the mural in the dining room. He wanted things done his way—too bad for him, he wasn't in charge. Holding her hands up for quiet, Jenny felt as if she were refereeing a fight between second-graders. "That's it. Lena, thanks, you're doing a great job. Just get back to it, okay?"

With muttered agreement, the woman did go back to work, throwing one last fulminating glare at the man smirking at her.

Jenny lowered her voice when she spoke again. There was no need to humiliate the man, but she wasn't going to be ignored, either. "Tony, you agreed when you signed on to this project to follow the planned art designs."

"Yes, but—"

"And," Jenny said, a little more loudly, "whatever you think of video games, the guests who will be coming to this hotel know these games like the backs of their hands."

Tony sighed heavily again. "If you'll only let me show you what I mean—"

"So," she said, overriding him again, "you will either do what you agreed to do, or you can pack up your paints and leave."

Insulted, he jerked his head back and glared at her. "You can't fire me."

"Oh, yes," a deep voice sounded from behind her. "She can."

Jenny looked over her shoulder, unsurprised to see Mike coming up behind her. The man was always close at hand these days.

"Mr. Ryan..."

Mike shook his head and continued speaking to the artist. "But allow me to repeat it so you'll understand. Either follow the planned design, or leave and we'll send you your last check."

"I'm an artist," Tony said hotly, lifting his chin with its wispy goatee. "If all you want is someone to fill in the lines with color, you don't need an artist. You need a child with a box of crayons."

"Your choice," Mike said. "Thanks for your time."

Clearly outraged, the man flushed darkly, then spun around to pack up his supplies, muttering all the while. From the corner of her eye, Jenny saw Lena do a little hip-shaking happy dance at the other artist's exit and she smiled.

"Well, that was fun." Jenny looked up at Mike. "I was handling it, you know."

"I saw and you were doing a great job." He smiled at her and Jenny's foolish heart gave a hard thump in response. "Any reason why I shouldn't help out when I can?"

"I suppose not," she said, but inside, she whispered that it wasn't a good idea for her to learn to depend on his help. Because it wouldn't always be there.

"Lena, are you all right here on your own?" Jenny asked.

"Are you kidding?" She laughed. "With Tony gone, it'll be like a vacation."

"Great. I'll send Christa up to help you when she finishes in the dining room."

"Fab, thanks. Oh, boss?"

Jenny and Mike both answered, "Yes?" Then Mike waved one hand as if telling Jenny to take it.

"I had an idea I wanted to run by you."

"Shoot."

Another grin from Lena. "I was thinking, what if I drew out one or two of the banshees so that their arms are stretched across the door—you know, so their clawed hands look like they're reaching for the guest opening their door..." She bit her lip and waited for a decision. She didn't have to wait long.

"That's a great idea," Jenny said and glanced at Mike. "What do you think?"

Nodding, he said, "I love it. Good thinking, Lena."

"Thanks."

"And your banshees look like they stepped right out of the game, I appreciate that," Mike added.

"Hey," Lena said, "I love that game!" When she turned to go back to work, humming to herself, Jenny and Mike headed back down the hall.

"The elevators are turned off, so we have to take the stairs."

"Yeah," Mike said, "I know. But I don't like you climbing up and down those stairs every day. What if you tripped and fell?"

"What am I, ninety?" Jenny shook her head and laughed to herself. "You're being ridiculous, Mike."

"I'm being concerned, Jenny," he said, pulling her to a stop just inside the stairwell. "I care about you. About our baby."

Care was such a pale word. It was pastel when what she wanted was bold, primary colors.

"I appreciate it, but we're both fine and I've got to

get downstairs to finish the main-floor elevator doors. We're one artist short now." She started for the stairs, but Mike was too quick for her. He scooped her up into his arms and Jenny huffed out a breath of exasperation.

He was smiling at her, holding her, and though she wanted nothing more than to hook her arms around his neck and hold on, she knew she couldn't. "You're not playing fair, Mike."

"Damn right, I'm not," he agreed, walking down the stairs with her held close to his chest. "I've told you how it's going to be between us, Jenny. I'm just giving you time to get used to the idea."

Later that night, the construction crew was gone for the day and most everyone else had headed into Laughlin for dinner and some fun. In the quiet darkness, Jenny went out onto the pool deck by herself, eager for a little solitude. It had been days now since Mike showed up at the hotel and it looked as though he had no intention of leaving anytime soon. Didn't he know that by staying, he was making this whole situation so much harder on her?

"Of course he does," she whispered wryly. "That's his plan, Jenny. He's trying to make you crazy enough that you'll agree to marry him, even though you know it would be a mistake."

Oh, God, she was so tempted to make that mistake.

Shaking her head at her own foolishness, Jenny sat down on the edge of the pool, took off her shoes and dangled her feet in the warm water. It was still cool in the desert at night, so she enjoyed the mix of a cold wind brushing over her arms and the warm water lapping at her legs. Lazily kicking her feet through the water, she leaned back on her hands and stared up at the night sky.

"Beautiful," she said to no one. With no light pollution here, the stars were brilliant and there were so many of them. It was like a painting, she thought and instantly, her mind drifted to just how she would capture that scene on canvas, though she knew she would never be able to do it justice.

"It is, isn't it?"

Jenny sighed and tipped her head down to watch Mike come toward her. Her time alone was over and though she knew that spending time with Mike was only prolonging the inevitable, she relished the hard thump of her heart at the sight of him. She'd thought he went into town with the others, but she should have known better, she told herself now.

He took a seat beside her, dropped his bare feet into the water and looked up at the sky. "Being in the city, you never see this many stars," he said, voice low, deep, intimate. "You forget how big the sky really is."

Jenny knew he hadn't come out here to talk about the stars. "Mike…"

He looked at her and in the shadowy moon and starlight, his blue eyes looked dark, mysterious. "I talked to Dave today," he said, surprising her. "He says you quit your job as of this project's completion."

Jenny had hoped he wouldn't find out so quickly. Turning in her resignation had cut at her. She loved her job and would miss everyone there, but she'd felt obligated to give Dave as much time as he might need to cover her absence. "I had to."

"No, you didn't," he mused quietly, sliding his bare foot along her leg, giving her chills that had nothing to do with the cool night air. "Dave also said you recommended he hire Christa full-time."

She shrugged. "He'll need someone to fill in for me when I'm gone. Christa's good. Talented, but willing to take direction."

"If you think she'll work out, that's good enough for me."

Pleased that he thought so highly of her suggestion, she smiled briefly. "Thanks for that."

"You could have stayed with the company, you know." He tossed a quick glance at the sky, then shifted his gaze to hers again. "Could have pulled the the-boss-is-my-baby's-father card."

She stared at him, shocked. "I would never do that."

His gaze moved over her face as he slowly nodded. "Yeah, I'm getting that. I'm beginning to get a lot of things."

"Mike," she said, hoping to make the situation perfectly clear between them. "Quitting my job was the right thing to do. For both of us. Working together every day would just be too hard. Besides, I don't need your money to take care of my baby. I don't need the Ryan name to make sure my future's secure—"

"What *do* you need, Jenny?"

Oh, wow, that question had too many answers. Too many pitfalls should she even try to tell him what was in her heart, her mind. So she smiled and said softly, "Doesn't matter."

"It does to me," he said.

Tipping her head to one side, she looked at him and asked, "Since when, Mike?"

"Since I woke up and started paying closer attention." He took her hand and smoothed his thumb across the back, sliding across her knuckles until she shivered at the contact. "I want you, Jenny. More than anything else in my life, I want you with me."

Her breath caught in her chest and her heartbeat quickened until it fluttered like a deranged butterfly. To be wanted. It had been the driving force in her life since she was a child. But now, she knew it wasn't enough. *Want* wasn't *love*.

"You do for now, Mike," she said quietly. "But what about in five years? Ten?" Shaking her head, she continued, "Want, need, passion, they're all good things. But without love to anchor them, they fade and drift away."

"They don't have to." He gripped her hand even tighter. "Love is something I've avoided, Jenny. Too big a risk."

She could see what it cost him to admit that, but with her heart hurting so badly, she couldn't tell him that she was all right and that she understood. "It's worth the risk, Mike. Because without love, there's nothing."

"Need is something. Want is something."

"But not enough." Sadly, she pulled her hand free of his, swung her legs out of the water and stood up. Looking down at him, she took a breath and braced herself to give him the hard truth she was only just accepting. "We have a child together, Mike. But that's all we have."

She walked back to the hotel and stopped in the doorway to look back at him. He was alone in the starlight, watching her, and it took everything Jenny had to keep walking.

Two days later, things were still tense between Mike and her. She had hoped that after their last conversation at the pool, he would give up and go home. He had to know that nothing was going to come of this. They each needed something from the other that they couldn't have. Jenny needed Mike to love her. To trust her. Mike needed her to settle for less than she craved.

Her time here at the hotel was almost done. Most of the paintings were completed now and what was left, Christa and Lena could finish on their own. Jenny couldn't stay much longer. Because Mike refused to leave her side, she had to be the one to leave. She had to get some distance from him before she did something stupid like rush into his arms and accept whatever crumbs he was willing to offer.

The cacophony of sound at the hotel was familiar now and Jenny half wondered if the silence of her apartment once she was home again would feel stifling. Between the men talking, the tools buzzing and crashing, and the roar of Jet Skis on the river, it was hard to hear yourself think. But in her case lately, maybe that was a blessing.

"Jenny! Jenny, where are you?"

Up on the second-story landing, Jenny was just adding a few finishing touches to the naked tree sprawled across the elevator doors when she heard that familiar voice booming out over the racket.

"Uncle Hank?" she asked aloud. Setting her paintbrush aside, she quickly went down the stairs and spotted her uncle, Betty right beside him, taking a good look around the front lobby.

"There she is," Betty shouted over the construction noise and used her elbow to give Hank a nudge in the ribs for good measure.

The older man's face brightened as he grinned and came toward her.

"Uncle Hank, what're you doing here?"

To her surprise, the usually stoic man gave her one hard hug, then let her go and beamed at her. "Well, Betty and I wanted to see what you were doing out here. Take a look around and see what's what."

"Darn fool, we could have caught a plane," Betty said, scraping her hands across her tangled hair. "But no, he insisted on driving so he could try out his new toy."

"No point in having a new car if you're not going to drive it," Hank pointed out.

"New car?" Jenny looked out the front window and saw a shiny red convertible. She couldn't have been more surprised. Though he was a wealthy man, Hank had been driving his classic Mercedes sedan for twenty years, insisting he didn't need anything new when that one ran just fine. Shifting her gaze back to her uncle, she asked, "That's yours?"

"It is," he said proudly.

"Like to froze me to death, driving out here with the top down the whole way," Betty muttered.

"No point in having a convertible if you keep the top up," Hank argued.

Jenny just laughed. It was so good to see them; she was enjoying their usual banter. But she had to ask, "You didn't drive all the way out here just to look at my paintings, did you?"

"Well," Hank hedged, "that's part of it, sure." His eyes narrowed on something behind her and without even looking, Jenny knew who was coming up beside her. Her uncle's features went cold and hard as Mike stopped alongside Jenny.

"Mr. Snyder," Mike said with a nod.

"Ryan." Hank gave him another narrow-eyed stare, then shifted his gaze to Jenny, ignoring the man beside her completely. "Jenny, I came to tell you I've sold Snyder Arts."

"What?" Stunned and in shock, Jenny stared at the man who'd raised her. First a convertible, now *this*? His company had been Uncle Hank's life. He lived and breathed the business, dedicating himself to building Snyder Arts into a well-respected, multimillion-dollar firm. She couldn't imagine him without it. "Why would you do that? You loved that business."

Still ignoring Mike, Hank moved in on her and dropped both hands on her shoulders. "I love *you* more," he said and Jenny received her second shock of the day.

He'd never said those words to her before and until that moment, she hadn't been aware of how much she'd wanted to hear them.

"Uncle Hank…"

"I see tears," he blurted and warned, "don't do that."

She laughed and shook her head. "I'll try. But tell me why."

"Main reason?" he said, sliding an icy glance toward Mike. "So no one could accuse you of being a damn spy for me."

"Damn it," Mike muttered from beside her.

Jenny hardly heard him as she stared into her uncle's sharp blue eyes. Oh, God. Guilt reared up and took a bite of her heart. He'd given up what he loved to prove something to Mike and it was all for her sake. "You shouldn't have done that," she whispered.

"It was time," Hank said, pausing long enough to glare at Mike.

"There's more to it than that," Betty interrupted, her

clipped tone cutting through the sentiment that was suddenly thick in the air.

Stepping in front of Hank, Betty looked at Jenny and said simply, "It was long past time he sold that business. Haven't I been trying to get him to live a little before he dies?"

"Who said anything about dying?" Hank wanted to know.

"Nobody lives forever," Betty snapped, then focused on Jenny again. "With the company gone, we'll both have time to help out when the baby comes. We can both be there for you, Jenny. And that's the important thing. Family stands for family. You understand?"

"I do," Jenny said and reached out to hug the woman who had always been a constant in her life. Heart full, she looked at the older couple and realized that she'd always had family—she'd just been too insecure to notice. Now, she couldn't understand how she had ever doubted what these two amazing people felt for her.

"Now, you just show us around," Hank said, letting his gaze slide around the lobby and briefly rest on her entry wall painting. "Let us see what all you've done here, then you can quit this job and come home with us where you belong."

She opened her mouth to speak, but Mike cut her off.

Speaking directly to Hank, he said, "I know you've got no reason to trust me, but I need a minute with Jenny."

"Mike—" She didn't want more time alone with him. Didn't think she could take much more.

"I think you've said plenty already," Hank told him.

"I agree with Hank," Betty said, lifting her chin imperiously.

"Please," Mike said, looking at Jenny directly, catching her off guard with the quietly voiced plea.

In all the time she'd known him, Jenny had never heard him say *please* to anyone. And that one simple word decided it for her.

To her uncle, she said, "I'll be back in a minute." Then she turned, walked into the game room, which was currently unoccupied, and waited for Mike to join her.

With so much happening, Jenny's heartbeat was fast, her mind spinning. She hardly knew what to think. Her uncle selling the company, her quitting her job, having a baby. And now Mike, wanting to talk again when they'd already said both too much and too little to each other.

She tried to calm the jumping nerves inside her by focusing on the view out the window. The desert landscape was softened by the trees swaying in a soft wind. Jenny focused her gaze on the purple smudge of mountains in the distance and tried to steady her breathing.

"Jenny?"

She turned to face him and her heart raced. He looked—unsure of himself. Something she'd never seen in Mike Ryan. That realization shook her. She wouldn't be persuaded, in spite of her instinctive urge to go to him and hold on until she eased whatever was bothering him.

"I feel like an idiot," he muttered, scraping one hand through his hair.

"Not what I expected to hear," she admitted.

"Oh." He laughed, but there was no humor in the sound. "There's more." He took a step closer, then stopped, as if not trusting himself to get within reach. "I can't believe your uncle showed up out of nowhere," he muttered.

"You're upset about Uncle Hank coming to see me?"

"Not the act," he said, "just the timing."

Now she was really confused.

"You should know that I was wrong about you. Right from the beginning, I was wrong and I think somehow I knew that, I just couldn't admit it," he grumbled in irritation. "Just like I know I've loved you from the first moment I saw you in that bar in Phoenix."

Suddenly unsteady, Jenny reached down and grabbed the back of a chair for support. *He loved her.* She hadn't thought to ever hear those words from him. Only yesterday, that confession would have had her glowing in happiness. Now, though, it was too late. "Mike—"

"Just hear me out," he said, moving in close enough to touch her. To hold her. Hands at her waist, he spoke more quickly now, as if afraid she'd stop listening. "I'm asking you to marry me, Jenny. Not *telling* you, *asking* you. It's not for the baby's sake, or convenience or any other damn reason except that I love you. I want to go to bed with you every night and wake up beside you every morning." His eyes locked with hers and she read the truth there and wished, so wished he had said all of this sooner.

"You're it for me, Jenny," he confessed. "Maybe that's why I fought it so hard. Seeing your future spilling out in front of you can be…overwhelming. But the thing is, no matter how I looked at the future, you were there." His hands tightened on her waist and the heat of his touch slipped inside her. "There is no future without you, Jenny. There is no *me* without you."

Her mouth worked, but anything she might have said was choked off by the river of tears crowding her throat.

"I need you to believe me, Jenny," he said urgently. "I love you. I trust you. Please marry me."

Oh, God, it was everything she'd ever wanted. The

man she loved was giving her the words she'd yearned to hear and it was too late. How could she ever believe in him when it had taken her uncle selling his company to make him believe in her? What kind of irony was it that she was given exactly what she longed for and couldn't have it?

Disappointment rose up inside her and she couldn't keep it from spilling out. "No, Mike, I won't marry you. I can't. You're only saying this now because Uncle Hank gave you proof your suspicions about me were wrong."

"No, that's not true."

She shook her head wildly. "I wish you had said all of this before Uncle Hank arrived. It would have meant everything to me."

"This is what I meant about Hank's timing. I was going to talk to you tonight." He shook his head and laughed ruefully. "I had it planned. Moonlight, seduction, romance…"

"Mike, you're just saying this now, to try to make it better."

"No, damn it." He scowled. "You're wrong. I believed before today. It was that talk the other night, out at the pool?" He pulled her tight as if expecting her to make a bolt for escape. "It was then reality crashed down on me. When you said you didn't need me. Didn't want my money. When you made me see that you're not the kind of woman who has to *trap* a man into anything.

"You're one of the strongest women I've ever known. You're beautiful, talented. You're kind and funny and you don't take any of my crap."

She laughed, but it hurt her throat, so she stopped short.

"You're everything to me, Jenny. You have to believe me."

"I want to," she admitted. "So much."

He smiled, just one brief curve of his mouth. "Then let this convince you." Digging into his pants pocket, he pulled out a small deep blue velvet box.

Jenny's eyes went wide and she sucked in a gulp of air and held it. He was telling the truth, she thought wildly. He'd already had a ring for her when Hank showed up. It was real. It was staggering.

Mike flipped the top of the box open, and showed her a canary yellow diamond, glittering in an old-fashioned setting that seemed to Jenny as if it were made especially for her. "When did you—"

"Yesterday," he said. "After our talk the night before last, I drove into Vegas, found the best jeweler in the city and got this ring for you." He lifted her chin with the tips of his fingers until her teary eyes met his. "I knew, before your uncle showed up, that I love you. I trust you. I need you, Jenny. I always will."

"Mike…" Her bottom lip trembled.

Taking her left hand in his, he slid the ring onto her finger and sealed it there with a kiss. "Say you'll take the ring, Jenny. And me."

It was a gift, Jenny told herself. A gift from the universe, because suddenly she had everything she'd ever wanted most in her life. She looked up into his beautiful eyes and saw her own love shining back at her.

"Jenny?" he asked, a half laugh in his voice, "you're starting to worry me…"

"There's no need, Mike. I love you. I have since that first night in Phoenix." She went up on her toes and kissed him lightly. "I'll take the ring. And you. And I promise I will love you forever."

"Thank God," he whispered and pulled her in close.

His arms wrapped around her, her head nestled on his chest, she heard him say, "You are the best thing that has ever happened to me, Jenny Marshall, and I swear I will never let you go."

Epilogue

A few months later, the wedding was held at the Balboa Pavilion. Built in 1905, the Victorian-style building was on the National Register of Historic Places, and a California landmark. The grand ballroom boasted dramatic floor-to-ceiling windows that provided a spectacular view of one of the largest small-yacht harbors in the world.

Candles flickered on the linen-draped tables scattered around the wide room. Yellow and white flowers decorated every surface and cascaded over the front of the bride-and-groom table. And tiny white fairy lights sparkled and shone on every window as the day wore down and night rushed in.

"It was all perfect," Jenny mused, leaning back against her brand-new husband.

Mike's arms wrapped around her middle, his hands

tenderly cupping the bump of their child, and he dipped his head to kiss the curve of her throat. "It was, and you are the most beautiful bride ever."

Jenny did feel pretty in her white off-the-shoulder dress that clung to her bosom and waist, then fell in a soft swirl of skirt to the floor. Mike, of course, was gorgeous: tall, handsome and looking as though he'd been born to wear a tux.

"I love you," she whispered, tipping her head back to look at him.

"Never get tired of hearing that." He grinned, kissed her and swore, "I love you, too. And I'm going to show you how much every day of our honeymoon."

A slow, knowing smile curved her lips. "You haven't had a vacation in years. I can hardly believe we're taking a week in Ireland *and* a week in London."

"And," he teased, "another week in Tuscany."

"Really?" Jenny turned in his arms and hugged him. "You didn't tell me!"

"Surprise!" He grinned down at her and said, "An artist really should tour Italy, don't you think?"

"Absolutely." Jenny couldn't possibly be happier, she thought. A man who loved her, a baby on the way, a job she loved and so many friends who had come to wish them well.

"Maybe we'll look around, see if we can find a spot we like, buy a place of our own there."

"Seriously?" He shrugged. "Why not? We can take the kids there every summer."

"Kids?" she repeated, still grinning.

"Well, we're not gonna stop at one, are we?" He patted her belly and she caught his hand and held it in place, linking the three of them.

"No, we're not," she agreed, then leaned back against him and watched their guests dance on the wide wooden floor beneath thousands of tiny white lights.

"Your uncle and Betty look like they're having fun," he said, giving a nod toward the dance floor.

Jenny smiled to see Hank and Betty dancing together, alongside Mike's parents. The four of them had hit it off well enough that they were all planning a trip to wine country together. Their family was big and growing, Jenny thought, and she couldn't be happier.

"You two should be dancing," Brady said as he and Aine approached. Their infant son had stayed home in Ireland with Aine's mother, and though of course they were worried about leaving him, they were also enjoying the little break from parenthood.

"Why aren't you?" Mike asked with a laugh.

"We're about to," Brady assured him with a slap on the shoulder. "But first, we wanted to say happy wedding, happy life and good luck with the baby."

"Thanks," Mike said and pulled his oldest friend into a hard, one-armed hug.

"What's all this?" Sean asked as he walked up to join them. "People partying without me?"

"Where've you been?" Mike demanded. "You disappeared like an hour ago."

"On the phone with the contractor from hell," Sean muttered, glaring down at the phone so he didn't see the amused glances Mike and Brady shared.

"How is the very efficient Kate?" Brady asked.

"Driving him crazy," Mike offered.

"Hey, you try dealing with a know-it-all," Sean quipped.

"We do it all the time," Aine said, with a grin for Jenny.

"She's right," the new bride agreed.

"All right, enough of the insults." Brady pulled his wife onto the dance floor and her delighted laughter spilled out in her wake.

"Can I dance with the bride now?" Sean asked.

Mike strong-armed him out of the way. "Get your own girl.

"You owe me a dance, Mrs. Ryan," Mike said and spun Jenny into his arms and then around in a tight, fast circle.

"Sweep me away, Mr. Ryan," Jenny said and laughing, she wrapped her arms around his neck and held on tight. While the music played and the night wore on, joy shone as brightly as the fairy lights in the darkness.

* * * * *

If you loved A BABY FOR THE BOSS,
don't miss the other stories in the
PREGNANT BY THE BOSS *trilogy*
from USA TODAY *bestselling author Maureen Child*

HAVING THE BOSS'S BABY
Available now!

And
SNOWBOUND WITH THE BOSS
Available March 2016!

And pick up these other fun and sexy reads from
USA TODAY *bestselling author Maureen Child*

DOUBLE THE TROUBLE
THE FIANCÉE CAPER
THE COWBOY'S PRIDE AND JOY
AFTER HOURS WITH HER EX

If you're on Twitter, tell us what you think
of Harlequin Desire! #harlequindesire

COMING NEXT MONTH FROM

HARLEQUIN *Desire*

Available February 2, 2016

#2425 His Forever Family
Billionaires and Babies • by Sarah M. Anderson
When caring for an abandoned baby brings Liberty and her billionaire boss Marcus closer, she must resist temptation. Her secrets could destroy her career and the chance to care for the foster child they are both coming to love...

#2426 The Doctor's Baby Dare
Texas Cattleman's Club: Lies and Lullabies
by Michelle Celmer
Dr. Parker Reese always gets what he wants, especially when it comes to women. When a baby shakes up his world, he decides he wants sexy nurse Clare Connelly... Will he have to risk his guarded heart to get her?

#2427 His Pregnant Princess Bride
Bayou Billionaires • by Catherine Mann
What starts as a temporary vacation fling for an arrogant heir to a Southern football fortune and a real-life princess becomes way more than they bargained for when the princess becomes pregnant!

#2428 How to Sleep with the Boss
The Kavanaghs of Silver Glen • by Janice Maynard
Ex-heiress Libby Parkhurst has nothing to lose when she takes a demanding job with Patrick Kavanagh, but her desire to impress the boss is complicated when his matchmaking family gives her a makeover that makes Patrick lose control.

#2429 Tempted by the Texan
The Good, the Bad and the Texan • by Kathie DeNosky
Wealthy rancher Jaron Lambert wants more than just one night with Mariah Stanton, but his dark past and their age difference hold him back. What will it take to push past his boundaries? Mariah's about to find out...

#2430 Needed: One Convenient Husband
The Pearl House • by Fiona Brand
To collect her inheritance, Eva Atraeus only has three weeks to marry. Billionaire banker Kyle Messena, the trustee of the will *and* her first love, rejects every potential groom...until he's the only one left! How convenient...

YOU CAN FIND MORE INFORMATION ON UPCOMING HARLEQUIN® TITLES, FREE EXCERPTS AND MORE AT WWW.HARLEQUIN.COM.

HDCNM0116

REQUEST YOUR FREE BOOKS!

2 FREE NOVELS PLUS 2 FREE GIFTS!

H HARLEQUIN®

Desire

ALWAYS POWERFUL, PASSIONATE AND PROVOCATIVE

YES! Please send me 2 FREE Harlequin® Desire novels and my 2 FREE gifts (gifts are worth about $10). After receiving them, if I don't wish to receive any more books, I can return the shipping statement marked "cancel." If I don't cancel, I will receive 6 brand-new novels every month and be billed just $4.55 per book in the U.S. or $5.24 per book in Canada. That's a savings of at least 13% off the cover price! It's quite a bargain! Shipping and handling is just 50¢ per book in the U.S. and 75¢ per book in Canada.* I understand that accepting the 2 free books and gifts places me under no obligation to buy anything. I can always return a shipment and cancel at any time. Even if I never buy another book, the two free books and gifts are mine to keep forever.

225/326 HDN GH2P

Name	(PLEASE PRINT)
Address	Apt. #
City	State/Prov.	Zip/Postal Code

Signature (if under 18, a parent or guardian must sign)

Mail to the **Reader Service:**
IN U.S.A.: P.O. Box 1867, Buffalo, NY 14240-1867
IN CANADA: P.O. Box 609, Fort Erie, Ontario L2A 5X3

Want to try two free books from another line?
Call 1-800-873-8635 or visit www.ReaderService.com.

* Terms and prices subject to change without notice. Prices do not include applicable taxes. Sales tax applicable in N.Y. Canadian residents will be charged applicable taxes. Offer not valid in Quebec. This offer is limited to one order per household. Not valid for current subscribers to Harlequin Desire books. All orders subject to credit approval. Credit or debit balances in a customer's account(s) may be offset by any other outstanding balance owed by or to the customer. Please allow 4 to 6 weeks for delivery. Offer available while quantities last.

Your Privacy—The Reader Service is committed to protecting your privacy. Our Privacy Policy is available online at www.ReaderService.com or upon request from the Reader Service.

We make a portion of our mailing list available to reputable third parties that offer products we believe may interest you. If you prefer that we not exchange your name with third parties, or if you wish to clarify or modify your communication preferences, please visit us at www.ReaderService.com/consumerchoice or write to us at Reader Service Preference Service, P.O. Box 9062, Buffalo, NY 14240-9062. Include your complete name and address.

HDI5

"You have to make a decision about attending the Hanson wedding."

Marcus groaned. He did not want to watch his former fiancée get married to the man she'd cheated on him with. Unfortunately, to some, his inability to see the truth about Lillibeth until it was too late also indicated an inability to make good investment choices. So his parents had strongly suggested he attend the wedding, with an appropriate date on his arm.

All Marcus had to do was pick a woman.

"The options are limited and time is running short, Mr. Warren," Liberty said. She jammed her hands on her hips. "The wedding is in two weeks."

"Fine. I'll take you."

The effect of this statement was immediate. Liberty's eyes went wide and her mouth dropped open and her gaze dropped over his body. Something that looked a hell of a lot like desire flashed over her face.

Then it was gone. She straightened and did her best to look imperial. "Mr. Warren, be serious."

"I am serious. I trust you." He took a step toward her. "Sometimes I think…you're the only person who's honest with me. I want to take you to the wedding."

It was hard to say if she blushed, as she was already red-faced from their morning run and the heat. But something in her expression changed. "No," she said flatly. Before he could take the rejection personally, she added, "I—it—would be bad for you."

He could hear the pain in her voice. He took another step toward her and put a hand on her shoulder. She looked up, her eyes wide and—hopeful? His hand drifted from her shoulder to her cheek and damned if she didn't lean into his touch. "How could you be bad for me?"

The moment the words left his mouth, he realized he'd pushed this too far.

She shut down. She stepped away and turned to face the lake. "We need to head back to the office."

That's when he heard a noise. Marcus looked around, trying to find the source. A shoe box on the ground next to a trash can moved.

Marcus's stomach fell in. Oh, no—who would throw away a kitten? He hurried over to the box and pulled the lid off and—

Sweet Jesus. Not a kitten.

A baby.

Don't miss
HIS FOREVER FAMILY by Sarah M. Anderson
available February 2016 wherever
Harlequin® Desire books and ebooks are sold.

www.Harlequin.com

HDEXP0116

Turn your love of reading into rewards you'll love with
Harlequin My Rewards

**Join for FREE today at
www.HarlequinMyRewards.com**

Earn **FREE BOOKS** of your choice.

Experience **EXCLUSIVE OFFERS** and contests.

Enjoy **BOOK RECOMMENDATIONS**
selected just for you.

PLUS! Sign up now
and get **500** points
right away!

Earn
FREE
REWARDS
Join
Today!
HarlequinMyRewards.com

MYRI6R